the Aval Prince

VOLUME THREE

Copyright © 2024 Myranda V. Peterson

Cover art and interior illustrations © Myranda V. Peterson
House MVP Logo © Myranda V. Peterson
The Avat Prince: Tales of Arkania Skits © Myranda V. Peterson

Cartography brushes used in map artwork designed by Joel Pigou
https://www.gumroad.com/joelpigou

ISBN 9781957330075

First Edition Printed August 2019
MVP TV Edition Printed February 2024

Printed by IngramSpark in the USA.

House MVP
16 Thomas Patten Dr., P.O. Box 21
Randolph, MA, 02368

http://housemvpmedia.com

The text of this book is set in 12-point Adobe Garamond Pro.

The Empire of Arkania

For those who are still searching for their circle,
and a place to call home.

The Avat Prince

VOLUME THREE

WRITTEN AND ILLUSTRATED BY

MYRANDA V. PETERSON

TALES OF ARKANIA

To access locked skits for
THE AVAT PRINCE:

First, get reading!

When you see the word 'TV' at the end of a
sentence, it's time for a skit!

Illustrations are paired off with these pages.
Scan an illustration's QR code to access its skit.

Enter the password.

Enjoy the show!

(Don't forget to come back to keep reading the story!)

HOUSE MVP

Previously in The Avat Prince...

After escaping the slave traders at Adelle's home, Brent seeks out her cousin, Lemm. On the way, he's found by the same slave traders who'd nearly captured him at Adelle's farm.

Neil, an Arkanian man, saves him, but it soon becomes apparent that Neil is no Avat-sympathizer. Instead, he and his family intend to sell Brent off to a man named Yorc. After Brent is examined by the old man the transaction is all but secured. Yorc just needs a day to collect the funds for the purchase.

Despaired, Brent desperately tries to think of a way to thwart his own fate. Spying a house on the way back to Neil's, he escapes and hides inside. To his relief, the house is Lemm's. Brent explains his situation to him and, angered by his cousin's recklessness, Lemm vows to rescue Adelle and give Brent back to her.

The two hitch a ride to Peluma from the nearby town of Devon, but are forced to walk the rest of the way when the merchant driving them realizes that Brent is an Avat. They then cross paths with a group of vagabonds hoping to kidnap Brent and sell him off. But Lemm defeats them easily, fully earning Brent's trust and adoration.

Upon their arrival in Peluma, the two are just in time for a slave auction that will sell Adelle and the other Avats that she's enslaved with. The event is interrupted when a band of barbarians raid it.

In the chaos Brent is found by another half-Avat boy named Aaron, and is led to safety. An imperial spots them and fires an arrow at them both — but Adelle throws herself into its path, saving the boys' lives at the risk of her own.

The three, along with Lemm, escape with the barbarian raiders to their village, The Liberation Front of Taranis, on the outskirts of the Empire. It's there that Adelle succumbs to her wounds after having Brent promise her that he'll trust his rescuers.

Elsewhere the Emperor of Arkania, Koberius, has begun preparations for seizing his own "freedom"…

18

THE MORNING AIR smelled different up here, on this high hill above the village. Fresher it seemed, more relaxing…and so very peaceful.

Closing his eyes, Brent took a deep breath of the sweet-smelling air that sighed around him. Then with a slow and steady exhale, he reopened them and looked at the area he stood in.

Dawn's light was already peeking over the darkened mountains in the distance, its rays inching towards the grassy cliff that he stood on. Imbued with the golden glow of morning they struck the hillside, alighting it with a serene and heavenly ambiance that forced his eyes to narrow.

Caught in that illumination, the dandelion seeds that hovered around him shined, their fuzzy bodies burning like fireflies, and at his feet the dewy grass seemed to sparkle. It almost looked as if he was soon to be standing in the presence of an angel.

Or maybe, he already had.

Holding small, loose fists at his sides he walked forward, his gaze now fixed on a tall tree that stood at the crest of the mount.

It was an amari tree, a villager in Taranis had told him, indigenous only to this valley with a thick, voluminous trunk and flowered vines that hung from its drooping branches. In every gentle wind those vines trembled, loosing fuchsia petals that pivoted into the breeze. Some even bumped into dandelion seeds, which they clung to and embraced in a gentle, swirling dance into the valley.

Squinting through the glaring sunlight Brent halted beneath the swaying vines and dropped his eyes to a gray headstone that was placed beneath them. Tightening his fists, he curled his lower lip into his mouth and bit it.

He stared at the rock, wavering between the option of sitting in front of it or standing where he was. In the end, with another refreshing wind blowing past, he elected to stand.

"H…hi, Adelle." For a split second he tried to smile. But it barely lasted, barely flickered, before a lone tear collected in one of his eyes and glided down his cheek.

One week had passed since she'd been buried.

One week since he'd been assimilated into the village of Taranis as a result of her gift to him.

Already his attire had changed: he was dressed in shin-length, doranis-skin pants and an open, tasseled vest that was decorated with emblems he'd never known existed. It was even adorned with the strange circles that he'd seen on Lemm's mask back in his cabin, and he'd been given jewelry to complement it: jade stones and onyx, crafted beads of wood…The village healer, Khirsta, had even changed the bandages on his arm for him.

It'd been strange to him at first, wearing the foreign clothes and accessories he'd been given. But he was getting used to it, just as he was growing accustomed to some of the other things in the village.

For instance, no one treated him unfairly because of his ears, and all of the children had eagerly adopted him as one of their newest friends. There was always food and water and games, and he was even being educated in the schoolhouse.

He'd never thought that such a life of refuge could ever belong to someone like him.

And it was all because of her.

"U-um…I don't really know what I should say…" His eyebrows puckered and he peered off to the side. "But, um, you were right. I guess. Y'know?" He perked up a little and looked at the gravestone again. "I…I really like it here. The people are really nice…like you." The corners of his lips reached up to form a sad smile. "…But…I wish you could still…"

He trailed off, already numbed by the unspoken words of his

unfinished sentence.

Knitting his brow, he struggled to contain his mounting emotion and clenched two shaking fists at his sides.

"I…I wish you could…" He sniffed loudly and raising an arm, he worked to scrub away his building tears.

He couldn't cry. She had told him not to cry…

"I-I'm sorry…Adelle…" He sniffed and after roughly wiping his face with the heels of his hands, he looked to the grave marker again. "I-I know, I shouldn't be crying, but…" Losing the strength to stand, he slumped to his knees.

"I'm…I'm so sorry…Adelle…" He bowed his head, his eyes hidden by his messy bangs as tears rolled out of them. "I-if I hadn't…maybe if I hadn't shown up…you'd still be here…"

"This isn't your fault."

He gasped faintly, startled by how clearly her final words had suddenly rung in his thoughts.

How could she have forgiven him for this back then? How could this not have been his fault?

Never before had he done anything worth being mistreated for — he'd only existed.

But now, just this once, when his mere existence had actually led to the death of someone who'd actually cared about him…

He sniffed again, his entire body quivering beneath the force of his quiet weeping.

He wished she could still be here. He wished he could hold her hand and see her laugh and smile along with him and everyone else in the village.

But no matter how much he wished for it, no matter how hard he tried to envision it, he knew that she couldn't. She never would.

But even so, she hadn't hated him. In the end, she hadn't blamed him at all.

She'd never sided against him, and she was the only one that never had.

Not when he'd dug his bare hands into her food, or had cried in her stable, or when the slave traders had burned down her property…not even when she'd died.

And it was only because of that had she led him to more people like herself. More people that would never hate him because of his existence.

He sniffed quietly.

"I...I know you can't come back," he choked out, swiping his arm beneath his nose again. He sniffled, barely able to see through his cloudy, red eyes. "I know..."

For a moment he just sat there, fussing over his watery face until he at last managed to gain some kind of bearing over himself. With his sobs gradually fading, he let his arms flop into his lap.

"...I...I think...I know what I should say now," he said, his voice trembling, and he paused to properly regain himself. Thus he overcame his emotions, and he gave himself the chance to part his lips and say the words he should've said from the very beginning; words that he should've said as soon as he'd met her.

"Th-thank you, Adelle." His sky blue eyebrows drew together, crinkling his forehead as grateful tears flooded his vision. "Thank you..."

At that moment, he suddenly realized: there was no way for him to express how truly grateful he was to her. She'd done so much for him in such a short time, and he owed her so much for it. But for now...

"Thank you..."

That was all he could say.

Wiping his face again, he gathered himself and got to his feet. When his misty eyes were clear he started away, but stopped at the fringe of trees that led back to Taranis.

He turned, meaning to cast one last look at the resting place that was behind him. But instead he found himself looking past the amari tree, over the valley and towards the far-flung mountain range. There, he thought he'd seen the smallest flash of movement.

Maybe it was just a trick of the sunlight reflecting in his watery sight. Or, maybe it was the flash of a distant smile —

The smile of an angel departed.*tv*

ANGEL'S DEPARTURE
CODE: AMARITREE

With his hands interlaced behind his back, Brent paced at the very end of Taranis later that day, kicking at the dirt as he gazed into the wide valley that rolled out beneath him.

It was a vibrant field, boasting rich plains, far-flung mountains and fully clothed trees that shivered in the morning breezes. Pacing atop this hill he could see it all, from the closest neighboring mount to the farthest borders. He could even spot the wildflowers that were a few miles out, their petals decorating the uniform green of the pasture with splashes of yellows, reds and deep blues.

All of it was pleasing to his eyes, and soothing more so, because it all reminded him of how far removed he was from the city, even from the entire Empire. It was as if by moving into this tiny village, he'd been transported to a place that was a world of its own.

Taranis added to the landscape's beauty, too: built to follow the slope of a high-rising hill the wooden houses, fashioned with porches, stairs and slanted rooftops, were sturdy and comfortable, and dirt roads sprinkled with patches of grass weaved between them.

Only one of them, dubbed the main road, was connected to all the others. It followed the rise of the hill to the very tip of the village, where a building called the Main House stood to crown it.

The Main House was the largest structure in the entire village, with a wide porch, tall windows and balconies that jutted out of either of its sides. Announcements and meals for rescued slaves were given there due to its size, Brent had learned, and some of its rooms also served as meeting places for the auction raiders — the very same warriors that had whisked him away from Peluma.

The tall timber of a forest stood behind it, whence a glistening stream poured out. It flowed straight down the village's center, babbled past the Main House and trickled down the main road and into the valley. There, it widened into a river that coursed deep into the fields and connected to the lake somewhere within.

That was where the other children were that morning. Brent had seen them leave with some of the adults a while ago.

But he didn't want to go there.

In fact, he didn't want to leave Taranis.

Ever.

But still he found himself here, waiting for them at the end of the main road with his fingers loosely intertwined behind his back.

Periodically he glanced down into the fields, half-expecting and half-hoping to see his friends scurrying back home. But every time he looked, they weren't there.

At last he sighed and, dropping his hands, he glared into the enormous valley for one long moment, as if that could make his friends come back faster.

It didn't work of course.

He twisted his lip and after twining his hands behind his back again, he returned to his pacing.

"Waiting for someone, *yi'lim?*"

Brent spun and his eyes snapped up to find the face of the one who'd snuck up on him. It seemed that almost everyone in the village was capable of approaching without him hearing.

It was Chief Ivan who'd arrived, his kind, bearded face turned down to meet Brent's golden eyes.

Brent liked him. He was nice. He'd even adopted Brent into his home, which was near the Main House, since he didn't have anyone else to stay with.

Like Renthor, the chief addressed Brent with a term of endearment. According to Aaron, *yi'lim* was the Katruskik phrase for "little one."

"Why are you not with other children, at the lake?" the chief inquired.

"Because…I don't want to go." Brent faced away and rotated so that he was looking into the valley again. Then he sat down and rested his arms on his kneecaps.

"Mm…" Ivan moved to stand beside him and after lifting his pant legs a little, he sat down, too. "You do not like the swimming, then?"

Brent stopped to think that over. "No. I just…don't want to go."

Ivan studied him out of the side of his eye, and then he looked back into the valley. "…You know, Empire is very, very far from here," he said after a short lapse of silence. "The only people in this valley, are people of Taranis."

A smile showed through his thick, dark beard, and he watched as Brent's golden eyes slowly, but surely, fell from the horizon to settle on the road that led to the lake.

"There is no harm that can come to you here," Ivan went on assuredly, following his line of sight. "Is why we take children to the lake, when we can. Is very fun there."

Brent pressed his lips together, but he made no sound to show that he'd heard Ivan's words.

Still his mind whirred, triggered by the many things that he knew to be latched on to that three-letter word.

Fun.

It meant no fear. No anxiety.

Just laughing, and playing, and smiles…things that he'd seen so much of amongst the other children in Taranis.

He could still find that even if he stepped beyond the village's borders?

"I know that…it has been hard for you. For you to adjust after what has happened." Ivan looked at Brent's brooding profile again, and in his bright blue eyes there lingered a glow of sympathy. "I understand…if you do not feel up to leaving the village just yet." He patted Brent on the shoulder and then with a soft grunt, he pushed up to his feet.

"If I go to the lake," Brent spurted, just a split second before Ivan took his first step away, and the large man stopped to face him again.

Brent paused hesitantly, his absent gaze still fixed on the hills. "…If…if I go to the lake," he said again, "will you…come with me?" He twisted around to see Ivan, his eyes large and innocent.

Ivan seemed to study him for a moment, surprised by the request.

But then his amazement melted into a soft smile.

19

"H A, HA-HA — *whoa!*" Clinging to Ivan's rock-hard arm, Brent felt his stomach fall away as he was swung into the air. Grinning, he swung his legs in and out, drawing himself further from the ground and closer to the sky.

Ivan laughed with him and releasing his forearm, Brent dropped, his skinny legs pumping to keep from falling.

His skittering soon slowed to an average walk and he paused, waiting for Ivan to catch up. When he was closer, Brent hurried off again.

Journeying to the lake, at least in Ivan's company, wasn't as dangerous as he thought it'd be. He could still see Taranis, just at the peak of the road he and Ivan had descended, and with each passing second the distant sound of gentle laughter and splashing became more apparent to him. It was a hollow noise, rebounding faintly, and he guessed that the lake wasn't even as far away as he'd thought.

"This way?" He stopped and pointed in the direction that the river went. It was coursing off to the left, where it weaved towards a body of pine trees up ahead.

When Ivan nodded, Brent looked at the wooded area for a second. Then, he started towards it.

"Do you want to go ahead?" Ivan asked, noticing the deliberate pace Brent had chosen and the way he constantly glanced back at the chief.

Brent peeked back at him again. Then, he let his gaze pan across the open field that was between him and the forest.

Falling back a little, he shook his head.

As he retreated to Ivan's side, the village leader placed a hand on his head and tousled his hair.

By the time they'd reached the outskirts of the trees, Brent could distinctly hear the individual voices of his new friends. They were shouting out to one another and in between a pair of cries he heard a loud splash, tailed by a chorus of surprised laughter.

Staying on the path, he crossed between the tall pines. On the other side, he was met with one of the most marvelous sights he'd ever seen.

The valley lake, a vast body that extended as far to the east and west as the distant foothills, glistened beneath the morning sun. Although it was nowhere near as big as the ocean near Peluma, it had to be close — but in many ways, it was different.

For instance, the air didn't smell or taste of salt. Instead it was fresh, and it eased the earlier fears that had once consumed him.

The surface was also smooth like glass, permitting it to act as a perfect mirror for everything that encircled it. All of the trees, hills, mountains, and even the sky were reflected in it, and their likeness-es were projected in such full color and proportion that it was as if an entire, upside-down world existed in the water.

Eager to get a closer look, he hurried to the shoreline.

When near enough he bent towards it and peered into the lake, where he managed to perceive a faded image of the sky. A slew of countless pebbles were layered beneath it, but what interested him more was that in between those sights, he could make out the faint silhouette of a spiky-haired child staring up at him.

Intrigued, he leaned closer to his reflection, but at a shuffle of movement behind him he threw his eyes back to see Ivan stepping through the trees and onto the shore.

Just as quickly, he looked to his left upon spying movement in the corner of his vision.

"Look out below!"

Splash!

A jet of water skyrocketed when a thin, redheaded boy crashed into it, his body curled up into a tiny ball.

Around the liquid explosion a group of children threw their arms up to shield themselves, grinning or laughing excitedly.

Instantly Brent recognized them: they were Liam, Eklaire, Renée and Mekial. The redheaded boy, who was now poking his head out of the water with a loud gasp, was Aaron.

Liam was a uniquely pale Avat with short blonde hair and eyes that were so silver they were almost white. He was the quietest of the group and although Brent didn't know him very well, he at least knew enough about him to perceive that he had a knack for speaking with a deadpan expression.

He seemed highly intuitive and observant, making him the most discerning. He could also be very intimidating as well because, when paired with his eyes, his often empty expressions were imposing. (Truthfully, Brent had thought he was blind when they'd first met, and had only begun to see Liam's eyes as intimidating when he learned that he could actually see. More often than not, it felt like Liam could look right through him, or even into his mind.) According to the villagers he was a Northern Avat — an "albino", was the word they used interchangeably — as opposed to the Southern Avats who were darker and more prevalent throughout the Empire.

Brent had never heard such terminology before. But what he did find interesting was that Northern Avats generally had poorer eyesight and extremely sensitive skin. Their hearing, however, was far better than their southern counterparts. The only downside was that in conjunction with their lesser vision, they suffered from involuntary rapid eye movement. Liam was no exception, and Brent had noticed that he sometimes tilted his head in order to compensate for it.

As for his skin, one of the village healers had concocted a cream that would protect him from the harsh summer sunlight. It seemed to work well enough but Brent had heard that on days where Liam didn't apply it, he was the victim of sunburns and rashes within the hour, especially if it was stiflingly hot out.

Eklaire was the most jovial, with a creamy complexion, mismatched eyes of green and blue, and a head of short white hair that curled over her round ears.

Her hair was white because her mother was from the imperial province of Lenora, she'd explained when Brent had wondered why, like him, her hair was of a unique color. She also had a strange drawl, and often dropped the "g" at the ends of any word that had it and slurred the words "you all" together to make "ya'll".

She said she got that from her mother, too.

Renée was another Arkanian, with collarbone length hair that was dark and straight, brown eyes, and light brown skin. She was a curious child, but she never seemed to intrude on others' personal space, and she was a welcoming and caring character. She was quieter than Eklaire, but not as much as Liam, and after Aaron had been the first of the children to talk to Brent.

With her eyes fastened onto his head she'd said that his hair was "really cool", to which he hadn't known what to say. He'd never gotten a compliment before, after all.

She'd been standing rather close when she'd said it. It'd made his heart beat fast, and his cheeks had felt rather hot.

He still didn't get why that had happened.

Mekial was her younger brother. He was the youngest — seven years old, Renée had said — and he shared the same skin and eye color as his sister.

He was a hyper and happy boy, adoring his sister and the older children, and even though he wasn't in the lake with them he sat atop the small ledge that Aaron had just jumped off of, his little face split by a huge grin.

"Try and top *that,*" Aaron challenged, his bright blue eyes moving between his friends as he paddled away from the place he landed in.

He was the oldest out of all of them — twelve years old, while Liam was eleven and Renée and Eklaire were ten. After moving into Ivan's house, Brent had also learned that Aaron was his son. He was an adventurous boy and when it came to matters regarding the slave trade, he was the most ambitious person Brent had ever known.

"One day, I'm gonna be a slave auction raider, too," he'd told Brent on his first night in Taranis. "I'll be one of the best!"

Brent had wondered why that was a goal for him. But he didn't ask.

Presently, he approached the area that his friends were gathered, Chief Ivan trailing behind him, and as he got closer he noticed that some of his friends' parents were nearby.

The first one he saw was Xëri, Ivan's Avat wife. Most of her physique had been passed down to Aaron, particularly her little nose and wavy red hair. This latter feature was one that Brent had been surprised Avats could have, but Aaron had simply explained that it was a trait connected to Avats from the "eastern isles".

Immediately Brent had wondered if these isles were related to the "isle of Avat sanctuary" that Renthor had told him about so long ago. But when he'd asked, Aaron had confessed that he didn't know.

Xëri had been at the victory banquet the night that Brent had arrived, and had served food to him and all of the other new villagers. She was very sweet and motherly, and twice already he'd called her "Mom", much to his embarrassment. Once he'd even called her "Adelle" and, seeing his distress, she'd assured him that he had her forgiveness.

But that only made him more upset.

Xëri was also a part of what Brent had learned was called the head council, a unit of leadership within the village that consisted of men and women who'd been present since the founding of Taranis. It acted as both an advisory board to the chief as well as a circle of judges for complicated disputes, even crimes in rare cases.

Most of them were Southern Avats, with brown skin and silky black hair. But two of them shared Xëri's unique hair type, namely a bulky man who was known as Zi'qu, as well as a woman named Qibëra. Along with their unique appearance, Brent had sometimes caught them speaking in a strange tongue with Xëri, a language that Aaron told him was called Aionbo. It had a peculiar sound, fast-paced, and although Brent could figure out that there wasn't too wide of a variation between sounds and wording, the familiarity of the near-unintelligible jumble of phrases struck a chord in his mind.

It took him a while to discern why, but he eventually remembered that he'd heard the language several times before, from Renthor's lips while he'd been living in the city. In fact, he already knew a few phrases from the older Avat — most of them being swears that Renthor had expressly forbade him to repeat — but he had also learned the names of certain objects and places.

He was nowhere near fluent, which made fully understanding the conversations that Xëri and the other council members had quite difficult. But he was occasionally able to pick out some words, even questions. The word "Elder" seemed to come up often, although Brent had no idea who it alluded to.

"You'll learn the language eventually," Aaron had promised him. "Mom has me practice it a lot. She'll probably teach you, too, since you live with us now."

Isabel and Richter, Eklaire's parents, were at the lake, too.

Isabel's hair was white, like her daughter's, but unlike Eklaire's it was waist-length and plaited over her shoulder. She was a small, blue-eyed woman and when he'd first seen her, Brent had noticed that she had a rough scar that ran from the bottom of her jaw up to the lobe of her right ear.

He hadn't asked her why she had it, but seeing it triggered memories of the stories that Renthor had told him: tales of physical abuse and beatings, and of scarring and emotional mistreatment. He couldn't help but wonder if such a tale would explain her wound.

Richter was a brown-eyed man with brown hair. Unlike Isabel and Eklaire he didn't have any strange accent — at least, not one that was as strong. But, he still shared their extraordinarily friendly temperaments.

He was a fisherman, Eklaire had told Brent, and so he was a part of the group of men who often ventured near the source of the river to gather fish for the village in the summer. She'd also said that while she referred to him as her "Pa", he wasn't really her father.

"He helped me'n Mama escape someone who'd enslaved her fer helpin' Avats before I was even born," she'd said. "Him'n my Mama went'n got married after that."

At that moment he was engaged in conversation with Isabel, who was seated in the shadow of a low and leafy branch. He was sitting next to her, and it was only when Ivan's great girth became apparent in the corner of his sight did he look up.

"Morning, Chief," he greeted and having already followed his gaze, Isabel hailed him as well.

"Glad to see you decided to join us," Xëri called out, turning her face from the children to squint at her nearing husband. Her eyes dropped to Brent. "You, too, Brent."

"Brent came?" Renée twirled around in the water, strands of her wet hair wrapping around her chin.

"Water's nice!" Eklaire shouted as Brent approached the ledge that Mekial was seated on. She threw one of her arms up to wave, splashing Aaron in the process. "You gonna come in?"

"Can you swim?" Liam asked, stroking towards the ledge as Brent kneeled to examine the rippling waters.

Mekial looked in with him, but he leaned a bit closer until he could see his distorted reflection.

He smiled at himself.

"Careful, Mekial," Xëri called warningly.

He pulled back.

"I can show ya how to swim, Brent!" Eklaire offered, swimming forward so that she was treading water beside Liam.

After looking around, she grabbed a small rock that was jutting out of the lake's surface and relaxed her body so that she was floating. "Just go on and kick yer legs like this!" She started kicking furiously, splashing water everywhere.

Coughing, Liam squeezed his eyes shut and dove out of sight.

Brent leaned away.

Beside him, Mekial blinked when Eklaire's splashing made his reflection disappear. He tried to reach out and touch the water, as if that would bring it back.

"And that there'll getcha movin'!" Eklaire finished and she stopped kicking. Treading water again, she looked around. "Where'd Liam go?"

She turned, her heterochromatic eyes darting to and fro, and she whipped back around when Liam popped up behind her with a gasp.

She lurched back with a yell and nearly slipped into the lake's dark depths. "Dang it, Liam! Ya near scared me to death!"

"I didn't do anything," Liam said after wiping away the water that clouded his sight.

Bloop.

Hearing the weird sound, the two looked about.

Trusting his ears, Liam turned to a series of small rings that were growing right behind him.

Eklaire glanced around before she looked in the same direction.

Renée and Aaron heard the sound, too.

Renée's eyes leaped from the ledge, to the ripples that were expanding near Liam. Immediately, she realized what had happened.

"Mekial!" she cried, her eyes widening in panic.

"I got him!" Aaron shouted.

But before he could even move someone else dove into the water. They were so smooth that a splash was hardly made.

Frowning, Aaron's eyes jumped to the ledge.

Brent wasn't there anymore.

20

W HAT HAPPENED?!"
Aaron's eyes shot off to his parents as they neared the shore.

He glanced from the ledge, to the ripples and back to them. "I-I don't know —"

"Mekial fell in!" Renée burst hysterically.

"Brent went in after him," Liam added and he and the others watched as Renée swam this way and that before she dove beneath the surface.

She popped back up rather quickly. "I-I can't see them!" she cried.

Suddenly, a loud gasp sounded somewhere to the left, drawing all eyes.

It was Brent, his clothes bogged with water and his hair plastered to his face. He clambered free of the lake and in his arms, he carried what looked like a small lump of sopping wet cloth with brown feet.

The bundle shuddered, and with the calling of her sibling's name Renée hastened out of the water.

Xëri came next and as she approached, she untied the patterned apron that hung over her ankle-length dress.

Mekial, soaked through and through, choked and hiccuped between his sobs as Brent carried him out and offered him to Xëri's outstretched arms.

Cooing him softly, she wrapped him in her apron and embraced him, rocking him gently as she reassured him of his safety.

Behind her Brent flipped his bangs out of his eyes, his heart still racing from the adrenaline that had just shot through him.

"So you *can* swim," Liam concluded.

Brent turned to look at him.

No sooner had he done so were his eyes met with the sight of lashing black hair. Before he could fully identify it as Renée's wet locks, she wrapped her arms around him.

"You saved him!" she exclaimed, her embrace tight.

Brent broke free of her hold and stared at her, his eyes wide and cheeks on fire.

What was she doing?

"Ha, ha, ha!"

Renée spun at Aaron's laughter and pinpointed his grinning face.

"Looks like Brent thinks you've got cooties!" he teased.

"I don't have cooties!" Renée countered, scowling. "I'm just thanking him!" She rounded on Brent, who was still standing there stiffly and staring at her with a stunned look.

That was what she was doing? Thanking him?

Well, why in the world did she have to hold him to do that?

Eklaire's giggling ripped him out of his confusion. "Cooties," she laughed. "That's a funny word."

"What…" Brent eased up a little and he looked between them cautiously. "What're…'cooties'?"

His friends stared at him.

Aaron spoke up first. "They're infectious!"

"Infectious?" Brent echoed, frowning.

"Like a disease!" Eklaire piped up next.

"Disease?" Brent rounded on Renée. "You're diseased?"

"No, I'm not!" she cried, her shoulders rising, and she turned on Aaron and Eklaire indignantly. "Quit lying!"

"Lying…?" Brent's eyes revolved to the two.

They wouldn't lie to him. None of his friends would.

Would they?[tv]

"Okay, okay, that's enough!" Richter declared, striding towards

YOU SAVED HIM!
CODE: DARINGRESCUE

the group and he put a hand on Renée's shoulder. "No one here is diseased or has 'cooties'. Eklaire," he looked at the girl, "have you got something to say to Renée?"

Eklaire grinned sheepishly. "I'm sorry, Ren. I didn't mean no harm by it. Honest!"

"Aaron?" Richter turned to the redhead next, and upon feeling the man's eyes Aaron sank in the water so that his nose was just above the lake's surface.

When he spoke, the water bubbled above his lips. "Sah-blee."

Richter didn't look pleased.

"Okay, okay!" Aaron sprang up. "I'm sorry!"

Richter tipped his chin in acceptance and he patted Renée's shoulder. "You all right, kiddo?"

"Yeah." Renée nodded rather stiffly, but her lower lip was poking out a little.

"So, we're all buddy-buddy again!" Eklaire cheered, involuntarily slapping the water to stay afloat. "Woohoo!" She sneezed suddenly, a small nasal expulsion like that of a newborn.

Aaron rolled his eyes. "Mom, Eklaire's sick again!"

Xëri, still rocking Mekial's sniveling form, looked at the children over her shoulder.

Isabel took her eyes off of Mekial to do the same. "All right, you come on outta the water, now 'Klaire," she said, waving her arm in a beckoning motion. "I don't want you gettin' sick on me again."

"Aww, but Mama, I wanna swim some more!" Eklaire kicked a foot out of the water to balance herself out, and with one back-pedaling stroke she flipped over and started to swim around.

"Don't make me repeat myself, 'Klaire!" Isabel called to her again. "You're just gonna make it worse!"

"But Mama, I — *achoo!*" Eklaire stopped mid-stroke, offset by the force of her sneeze. Sniffing, she turned around with half-lidded eyes and her gaze met Liam's. Mucus was hanging out of her nostril.

He wrinkled his nose. "Ew. You have a booger."

Eklaire sniffed again and then, with a wide grin spreading across her face, she swam towards him.

"A-ah! Don't come near me!" He started swimming away.

Aaron laughed.

"Imma getchu, too!" Eklaire switched targets and swam in his direction.

"No!" He made to escape. "You're gonna get *me* sick!"

Back on the shore, Brent laughed and Renée giggled, her hands over her mouth.

"Ew, yuck!" Eklaire suddenly stopped swimming and wiped her face.

"What?" Aaron, having neared the shore, peeked back at her.

Liam, too, stopped swimming. "Did you just…swallow it?"

Eklaire finished wiping her face and giggled. "Almost did! Good thing I stopped myself!"

Liam looked away with a soundless closing of his eyes.

"Ugh!" Aaron exclaimed.

Renée giggled again. "You're so weird, Eklaire."

Eklaire smiled broadly.

"All right, Eklaire, time to come out," Isabel tried again as her daughter paddled around in a circle. "You just got over a summer cold!"

"Just five more minutes?" Eklaire begged, stopping to look at her. "Please, Mama? I almost never get to come down here!"

"That's cuz you always get sick!"

"*Please*, Mama?"

"…All right," Isabel relented and she planted her fists on her hips. "Five more minutes. But I'm gonna be countin' off, y'hear?"

"Yay!" Eklaire started swimming in circles again, and as she did her mother began to count.

"One…! Two…!"

"Brent, you should come in, too!" Eklaire burst over her, looking in his direction. "The water's nice!"

"Three…four…"

"Yeah, Brent!" Renée grabbed his hand with both of hers and started to pull him towards the lake. "You can swim after all!"

"Five! That's it, 'Klaire, I'm comin' to get you!"

"But Mama, that was only five seconds —!" Eklaire started to protest, her nearly invisible eyebrows knitting as she shifted her eyes to her mother.

Her face quickly opened in shock when she saw that Isabel was running right at her, splashing through the lake as she advanced.

Eklaire squealed excitedly, and she threw her arms up when Isabel leaped into the air. Tucking her legs into her chest she plunged into the lake, sending water jetting into the sky.

When she bobbed back up she reached her daughter in one smooth, forward motion, and with an animated cackle she grabbed her around the waist. "Gotcha!"

Her cheeks red with laughter, Eklaire giggled and squirmed in her mother's grip until she managed to wriggle free. She proceeded to splash her in the face.

Isabel only laughed with her and after ducking beneath her arm, she splashed Eklaire back.

Eklaire's giggling echoed around them as she started to swim away. "Ya can't catch me, Mama!"

"I'm comin' for ya, 'Klaire!"

As Isabel swam in pursuit, Aaron and Liam tore their eyes away in order to view the shore, whence a storm of splashing feet was sounding.

Their jaws flopped open at the sight of a hovering and grinning Ivan right before he crashed into the lake, creating such a massive wave that it actually carried them some distance away.

"I cannot let Isabel be only parent having the fun, huh?" he cried after popping out of the water and shaking wet hair out of his face. "Richter!" He turned around and waved a huge arm at him. "Are you coming?"

"Not today, Chief," Richter replied, spreading his hands. "Someone's gonna have to take care of those two when they both get sick."

Eklaire and Isabel engaged in a tickle fight, making water splash everywhere. It was only when they both sneezed did they stop, but then they burst into laughter.

"Watch out, Dad!"

Ivan glanced around when Aaron's voice broke out, and he chuckled as the boy crawled onto his back and proceeded to climb atop his shoulders. "What are you doing, son?"

"Climbing a mountain," Aaron answered casually and Brent watched, eyebrows raised, as the messy-haired preteen stood on

Ivan's shoulders, perfectly balanced. "Whoa…I'm so high up!"

"Not for long!" Ivan shouted and he swooped forward, making Aaron stumble and sway, his arms swinging.

Soon giving in he plugged his nose and dropped into the lake, spraying Liam with his splashing descent.

"Augh!" Liam rubbed his nose frantically and beside him Aaron slowly rose from the lake depths, spitting water out of his mouth like a fountain. "You got water up my nose!"

"Don't be such a baby," Aaron snorted and with a crazy grin Liam jumped on him, forcing them both under. By the time they popped back up, they were splashing and wrestling.

Cheering, Ivan spread his arms and jumped forth, belly-flopping so hard that they were whisked away in another tidal wave.

"Don't forget me!" Beaming vigorously, Renée dashed in after them.

By sheer instinct Brent took a few steps out to follow her, but he stopped when he was about knee-deep in the water.

Oblivious of him Renée leaped clear of the lake and dropped back in, her legs curled into her chest.

Brent stared at the spot that she'd fallen in, and he upturned his gaze in time to watch as everyone else joined in a game of laughing, splashing and diving.

Mesmerized by it all, his golden eyes glittered. Then, with his teeth flashing in pleasure, he laughed.

Suddenly, something launched out of the lake and coiled around his neck.

He started, stunned, and whatever had grabbed him used their weight as leverage to haul him into the water.

His instincts kicked in, ordering for him to free himself before the worst could happen. But he was pulled headfirst into the lake before he could try.

Cold water rushed him from all sides, and every noise that had once surrounded him became dull and muffled. Even the rush of a nearby movement was stifled.

Unable to identify it, he tried to find it. He barely spotted a pair of arms before they grabbed hold of him and pulled him to the surface.

He gasped loudly when he reemerged, wind blowing over his wet face and his hair once again clinging to his brow.

Flipping it out of his eyes, he glanced around and saw that he was much closer to everyone else than he'd been before. Now that he thought about it, he was even treading water.

Confused, he tried to figure out what had happened. In the process, he saw someone next to him.

It was Renée.

She smiled. "Gotcha!"

It dawned on him then: she'd pulled him into the lake.

At first he was offended. But then, he grinned.

"I'll get you back!" He splashed her.

She shrieked in excitement and took off, laughing as he pursued her.

But he was caught up by something — a huge arm — and with a yell he watched as the lake fell away from him. Soon, his entire body was freed from it and he peeked down to see that Ivan was holding him in the air.

"Fire one!" he boomed and he threw Brent skyward.

He yelled, shocked that Ivan would do that to him. But in the next instant, his cry melted into laughter.

Turning his eyes to the sky, he watched as it flipped over and under him, then over again.

"Fire two!"

Aaron went flying next, and Brent was airborne long enough to catch him somersault in midair before the lake consumed him. Bubbles clouded his sight then, all of them dancing around his sunken frame.

Another mass of them burst into existence a few feet away, Aaron cradled in their grasp.

They bounced back up to the surface together.

Just as they did, Ivan sounded off again, "Fire three!"

The next thing they knew, Liam was soaring towards them.

"And another!"

Renée came next, giggling spiritedly, and she and Liam crashed into the lake on either side of Brent and Aaron.

"Look out!"

Eklaire skyrocketed, gripping her toes as she spiraled towards her friends with a high-pitched cheer. With a dull slap she disappeared beneath the lake surface, and then popped back up a short distance away from where she'd landed.

"Get him!" Aaron shouted, pointing at his father, and screaming like an army he and his friends rushed the chief, attacking his chortling form with a barrage of combined splashing.

Envious of their entertainment, Mekial rolled out of Xëri's arms and ran to the shoreline, leaving the woman in her seated position beneath one of the lakeside trees.

But, due to his inability to swim as well as his older friends, he couldn't go out to them. So he stood knee-deep in the lake and knelt down to splash some of the water around.

Realizing that he wasn't having any fun, he stood up and gazed at them longingly. "I wanna play!" he whined. His shoulders sagged when he saw that no one had heard him.

Or so he'd thought.

Spying his little form in between her splashing, Renée swam towards him and climbed out of the water so that she was standing in front of him. Taking his hands in hers she started stomping, sending small shoots of water flying around her legs.

Catching on to what she was doing Mekial started stomping, too, and soon his stomping reverted to hyperactive marching, as if he was standing on a bed of hot coals.

Renée laughed and started hopping with him, her hands still clinging to his. But she stopped, her spine going rigid when a powerful wave of water hit her from behind.

With a startled gasp, she turned and her eyes fell to the two boys who'd swum near her.

Brent and Aaron grinned.

"Toldja I'd getcha!" Brent crowed and Renée playfully kicked water at him.

He and Aaron fervently retaliated, pushing up another impressive wave that caught both her and Mekial.

Declaring that she'd team up with her brother Renée kept kicking water at them, and they energetically continued to splash her and Mekial back.

Laughing loudly, her brother leaped in front of her and swooped his arms from his legs to the sky.

A towering wave of water followed the guidance of his hands, its bulging form growing out of the lake to darken a bewildered Brent and Aaron in its shadow. It swelled ever higher, blocking their view of the sky until, without warning, it crashed over them and submerged them completely.

Renée raised her eyebrows. When she looked down at Mekial, he faced her with a wide smile.

She considered him for a short second. "Uh…Mekial?"

Mekial just giggled.

Gasping, Aaron resurfaced several feet away from them.

Brent popped up shortly after and shook his hair out of his eyes.

"That…was weird," Aaron said at last, smacking one ear so he could pump water out of the other. "Who knew Mek could do that?"

"He practically drowned us!" Brent exclaimed. He rounded on Renée. "Is he an aetheriest?!"

"You're just a sore loser!" Renée teased spiritedly and she jumped when Liam snuck up on her with an impressive splash. She rounded on him. "Hey!"

He smiled lightly. "I came to even the odds."

"Way to go Liam!" His competitive edge reignited Aaron re-joined the fight, Mekial's strange act already gone from his mind.

Brent joined him.

Eklaire followed and splashed all of them.

They laughed anyway.

And in that moment, Brent felt a sense of gratitude well up in his heart. Ivan's words seemed true.

No harm could come to him in this valley.

⤙ ✤ ⤚

It was late in the afternoon when they finally began the return journey to Taranis. The trip had been delayed because Isabel and

Xëri had packed a few picnic baskets full of food for everyone.

The meal had consisted mostly of sandwiches that were filled with slices of meat and juicy vegetables. But there was also a home-made treat that Isabel called "Arkanian Prune Pie."

It was a cake-looking dessert that was made of Arkanian prune slices neatly layered atop a spread of sweet, fruity jelly. Holding it all together was a crust that was made of soft, honeyed bread.

The children and even the adults had eaten the naturally fla-vored snack but Brent had denied it, because he'd remembered what an Arkanian prune looked like. He settled for having half of Xëri's sandwich instead.

A short while after lunch, the adults decided that they were due to return home. The children were instructed to dry themselves off, which Brent's friends managed to do thanks to some heavy cloths that they'd each brought from home. Having come to the lake un-prepared, Brent had no such item to help dry himself.

Taking note of the boy's trouble, Ivan gave him his vest.

It was huge when it hung off of Brent's shoulders but it was soft and warm, and carried a distinct musk that reminded him of the fields in the valley. Grateful, he thanked the giant for his generous offer and used it to soak up the excess water that had gathered in his attire. He went to dry his feet next but then, thinking better of it, he simply took off his sopping slippers, opting to travel home bare-foot instead. The vest he returned to Ivan, who seemed surprised.

Brent didn't think to explain himself. He just hurried to meet with his friends before they could leave him behind.

Still, he could've sworn that he heard the grown-ups share a laugh as they gathered up the picnic baskets behind him.

He fell into step alongside Aaron and the others rather quick-ly, but he barely tread along the path for long before the feeling of dirt between his toes began to renew thoughts of a time that, now, seemed so very far away: one where his feet had been broken and crusted, and when following such a wide road would've lead him nowhere.

His eyes lowered, his gaze growing vacant, and he stared at an image that wasn't there: one of cracked earth beneath a scorching sun, distorting heat waves, endless, sandy hills —

"Race ya!"

Someone slapped him on the shoulder and blew past him in a blur, jerking him back to the present.

Right when he recognized them as Aaron three more people ran past, moving so fast that he was just barely able to identify them as Liam, Renée and Eklaire.

Mekial scampered by next. "Wait for me!"

Brent beamed and took off after them, running so fast that within seconds, the images of his troubling memories disappeared. And for the first time in years, he felt safe.

For the first time in years, he felt free.

21

S HAFTS OF LIGHT hung through the shadows, bleeding over Brent's head to line the cold, stone floor.

They were the first things that he saw when he opened his eyes, and they greeted him with a heatless glow that faded into the surrounding darkness.

He blinked. Hard.

The world sharpened into focus. But, it was all still dark.

Where was he?

Lifting his cheek off the floor, he tried moving.

Thump.

His foot hit a wall.

His head spun.

Glancing around, he sat up a little. Confusion was evident in the pursing of his brow.

He'd barely moved…why was the room so small?

He tried stretching again.

Thump.

He hit his elbow this time.

Again he paused, his thoughts aligning as his consciousness pieced itself together.

All at once, he realized that the shafts of light were falling across his body. He could see his clothes thanks to them.

But, strangely, they weren't his clothes from Taranis: his slippers were gone, to be replaced with sandals that wrapped his legs all the way up to his knees; his village trinkets had been relieved by thick bracers that cuffed his forearms; and his open vest was a white tunic hemmed with gold and scarlet thread.

He panicked.

Urgently, he flipped onto his side, his stomach, and examined himself all over, patting down his outfit as if it wasn't real.

But it was. He could feel the soft wool, the threading, the silk, the leather, the metal. These were all his clothes, his jewelry.

But…he hadn't worn any of it since…

Since…

Tensing, he looked up and around again.

This tiny space. These close-set walls. This light that fell into a small, tight area…

His heart dropped and his stomach melted.

Yes…he knew this place.

It was a closet.

He'd fallen asleep in this closet before, he recollected.

And…

And he'd dreamed.

Yes — countless times. In fact, every time he'd been thrust in here and had grown weary of screaming for someone to come back and free him, he'd cried himself to sleep.

At that, his mind ground to a halt. Even his breathing felt shallower.

Quietly, gently, he touched one of his eyes.

Something had crusted itself to his eyelashes. He scrubbed at it again before fully recognizing what it was.

Dried tears.

He stared at his hands.

He'd been crying earlier. And, if memory served, he'd eventually fallen into a fitful sleep.

But if that was true, then that would mean…

He raised his head to the shuttered door that barred him, feeling both horrified and sick.

This entire time…he'd been dreaming.

Again.

His chest tightened. All around him, the air suddenly felt stiff and cold.

That couldn't be right, he tried to tell himself. He couldn't have just imagined Adelle, and Lemm, and Chief Ivan, and Taranis. He couldn't have just imagined his friends, and the smell of the valley or the calm of the lake.

Or did he?

Because if he was here, stuck in this tiny closet that he thought he hadn't seen in three years, then that had to be exactly what had happened.

After all he'd had all sorts of dreams in this place before: visions of what the world might look like if he wasn't an outcast in his own home, of what his life might be like if he wasn't something as abominable and repulsive as an Avat.

That was why he'd always been sealed away in here, especially when company was due to arrive. His father had told him so enough times.

Because no one could know that the royal family had been tainted, marred by the presence of a goblin that dared to share their most telling traits of blue hair and bright, golden eyes.

Maybe it was a cruel trick of the imperial gods.

Or, perhaps it was just bad luck.

"I should just sell you off to the slave traders," his father had told him once before, his golden eyes carrying a malignant shine that had rooted Brent in place. "But because you still bear the marks of royalty, it would only result in a scandal. You remain under my care only out of my convenience. But as far as the world is concerned, *you do not exist.*"

Sometimes Brent had thought that he was lucky. He hadn't been entirely removed from his father's land, and he hadn't been surrendered to the temple priests, either.

But still…

Before his eyes the shafts of light blurred, morphing into fuzzy squares and circles that doubled across his vision. At the same time, something wet and warm rolled down his cheeks.

More tears.

Bowing his head, he pressed his hands into the floor and tried curling them into fists.

But they were trembling too much. He couldn't even see straight.

It made sense, if he thought about it. The world that he'd envisioned had been far too perfect to have ever been his reality. Even Renthor, the very first person that he'd met in the lumpy, trash-laden slums of the city, had been nothing more than a figment of his own overactive imagination. After all, even if he did arrive on the city streets, alone and desperate, no one would've gone out of their way to help him.

It was all just the pitiful hopes of a pitiful child. And hope had no place in the life of any Avat.

Sniffing, he swiped his arm beneath his nose.

Regardless of how bitter it seemed, he wished he could go back to that dream. But everyone had to wake up at some point.

Lifting his head, he peered through the slats of the door before him. Maybe it was the lasting rebellion of the light that still flickered within him, but he suddenly found himself struck by an alternative idea:

Was it possible that, somewhere in the world, the people he'd dreamt of really existed? Was it possible that, if he could somehow escape this tiny prison, he could find them in reality?

They'd felt so real to him, and even in this waking world he felt them near to his heart. That had to mean that they were real, didn't it? They'd felt real. So they had to exist somewhere.

And maybe they'd dreamt of him, too. Maybe, they were even waiting for him.

Somewhere...

Raising his arm, he slowly reached out for the door.

It was locked from the outside, he knew. But, if he tried the handle, or threw all of his weight against it, then —

His ears tingled, catching a strange vibration, and dust rained onto him.

Dropping his arm, he looked up.

More dust sprinkled down, and the ceiling rumbled softly.

With his eyes still pinned to the ceiling Brent got to his feet, using the wall for support. Across the tiny space, the shafts of light stretched across his face and caught the crown of golden feathers that encircled his head.

Once more his pointy ears shuddered, and the entire closet trembled when the building swayed.

A minute later, everything went still.

His ears rang in the quiet, in the silence. He swallowed, searching the air as if he could find the source of the disturbance.

Out of nowhere the room shook again and he stumbled, staggered. He caught his balance when it was all over.

But only for a second, for an instant later the walls shifted, the beams that framed the closet snapped and the whole room collapsed, meaning to bury him alive.

He shouted, terrified, and threw his arms over his head. The chaos inhaled his voice.

When it was all over he was lying flat on his stomach, his body tucked beneath several beams of wood and shattered stones. He counted it a miracle that he hadn't just died.

Shifting, he coughed heavily and shook his head. When his vision cleared, he saw that the darkness that had once contained him was now flooded with smoke. All of it was tinted by a fierce, orange light — the light of fallen torches and broken chandeliers.

Recovering his senses, he carefully shimmied out of the wreckage and got to his feet. At that point, he studied his surroundings.

What looked like a section of an upper floor of the mansion had flattened the closet entirely, burying it beneath broken columns, shredded imperial banners, and other decorum. There were even slabs of mosaic flooring, along with ripped pieces of a crimson carpet that was edged with gold.

Looking up and down the corridor revealed more such destruction, with slabs of flooring, capitals and fragmented statues littering the broken ground. It was as if a quake had ripped through the building itself, yanking almost everything on the upper floors into this underground level.

Through breaks in the ceiling he could see parts of the manor as well: red walls of plaster, oil paintings of political leaders, suits of armor, latticed windows and rib-vaulted ceilings…

Fire was dancing through all of it, and smoke was spilling into the basement by way of the new chasm in the floor. His eyes watered and his chest heaved; he coughed into his arm.

He had to get out of here, and fast.

Never mind his vivid dreams and hopes of a sanctuary that had only ever existed in his head. Never mind his wishes to see Adelle or to be with his friends.

Right now, in this very moment, he had to survive.

Somewhere down the hall, he heard a collection of stones tumble to the ground. Then, there came a soft exhale of breath — or perhaps a final sigh of release.

He turned towards it. "H-hello?" he called.

There was no answer.

With one arm pressed over his nose and mouth he moved down the passage. His shadow leaped against the walls every time he went past a fallen torch or through the remains of a fallen candelabra and his eyes stung, burned by the touch of smoke and growing fire.

Pushing through it all, he kept moving towards the sound that he'd heard. If he was lucky it was one of the manor's slaves, who would perhaps treat him fairly enough given their shared features and ranking in terms of racial hierarchy. Maybe they'd even help him get away from this place and whatever had caused the building to fall apart.

At least, he hoped they would.

"Hello…?" he called again and he stopped.

There was a break in the smoke up ahead, revealing what looked to be an intersection of corridors marked by smooth, plain columns.

Someone was standing in their midst, with their back to Brent and a sword in their hand. Firelight bounced off of the shifting smoke that hovered around him, and at his feet there laid the bodies of several soldiers.

Their eyes were pointed blankly at the ceiling, or at the walls, and pools of blood surrounded them, all shimmering in the glow of the fire.

Without meaning to, Brent gasped loudly.

The boy who stood among the corpses flinched, hearing him. Then, he began to turn around.

Brent only saw his glowing, golden eyes before he spun on his heel and ran.

But Koberius had already spotted him. Indeed, the sight of Brent hastening back into the smoke was vivid and clear in his sight.

He smiled eerily. "Well, then…"

Dragging his blade across the bloody floor, he started after the child at a slow and deliberate pace.

Huffing and puffing, Brent splashed through puddles of groundwater and darted around patches of idle flame. He didn't dare look back, didn't dare stop. Even with the smoke curling into his nose and lungs he kept moving, his arms and legs pumping as if his life depended on it.

With a pang of nostalgia and a rush of sorrow, he wished that Renthor was with him. He'd probably know what to do.

But, he had no one now. He never had.

So he had to fend for himself.

"*Where are you…?*"

The call was soft and listless, as if the speaker was floating through a dream. It came from somewhere behind him, and Brent instantly knew that it belonged to the boy he'd nearly ran into before.

Had he seen him? Was he after him?

Would he kill Brent next?

He didn't know, didn't even want to know. All he did know was that he didn't want to die.

Not here, where he was forgotten. Not here, where he'd been abandoned.

Not here, in this terrible world of fire, and smoke and neglect.

Pat…pat…pat…

The boy's footsteps were nearing him, drifting closer through the smoke and the fiery haze. The air seemed to thicken with each step that he took, weighing on Brent until every breath felt heavier than the last. His running slowed and he fought to catch his breath.

Behind him the boy called out again, still in that crooning tone of voice: "*Come out, come out…*"

Pat…pat…pat…

"*Wherever you are…*"

He chuckled darkly.

His chest heaving and his mouth dry, Brent dove around a corner and ducked into an archway that extended into another fiery hall. With gentle steps he backed into it, finding shelter in the very same shadows that he'd once feared.

His ears rang, latching onto the stillness. The boy's footsteps had ceased entirely.

He gulped.

At once, the skin on his nape crawled and a strange wind touched him from behind.

Then the boy's voice issued out to him, gentle and yet malevolent: "There you are."

Brent spiraled.

The boy was standing right in front of him now, as if he'd materialized. His indigo-blue hair was lashing, his lips were drawn back into a sneer — and his left eye was twice its normal size, with an iris that had swelled to fill the sclera, and a pupil that had stretched into a long, vertical slit.

Koberius' grin widened. "I found you…"

Brent thought to scream, but before he could Koberius snatched him by the neck and slammed him into the wall.

Stars blew across Brent's vision.

"Filthy *lookalike.*" Veins pulsed along the boy-king's arm, drawing attention to his unnatural strength.

He squeezed Brent's throat.

Brent gasped. He snatched at the boy's fingers to pry them off, but to no avail.

"To think," Koberius' gaze hardened and his slitted eye glittered, "that Çaru'qu believed I would let this happen again. When I'm this close to revival…"

Brent wheezed.

The emperor crushed his throat, cutting off his voice entirely. "This whole time, you were hidden here…right under my nose." He grinned and in the depths of his slit pupil, a red light became apparent. It was hard, if not impossible, for Brent to tell what it was shaped as. "But I can smell it, you know: your blood." His smile flattened into a hard and steely glare. "Tainted…by the *curser.*"

Brent pumped his mouth. Barely any sound came out.

His skin began to blue.

"I will" — flames amassed along the end of Koberius' sword and spiraled their way up to its hilt — "soak this realm in blood. And it will call to us…free us…!"

With his airways all but crushed, Brent's eyes rolled.

Someone…

"Greet Çaru'qu for me —"

Adelle…!

"— *spawn of Zion!*"

With a whirl of flame and eyes of vengeance, the emperor of Arkania went to stab his victim.

There was a flash of light, one like lightning, and the entire archway shook when something inhuman, something bestial and celestial, released a roar that could've toppled a mountain. The world spun out of control, the darkness wavered, the air unleashed a magnificent series of *pops* as if reality itself had been broken —

And memories, or maybe even faces, flashed through Brent's head: Adelle's, Lemm's, Ivan's; his friends; the villagers of Taranis —

Then there came sights and sounds that he didn't remember, didn't even recognize: a young man with trailing, sky-blue hair; that same man standing before a set of giants whose scaly, serpentine bodies towered over the land, over the world, over the sky; fangs and teeth and terrible wings; blasts of light and fire; bloodshed and land ripped asunder; swirling clouds of teal, and gold, and white —

A man in a mask with lion-like features and a wild mane of onyx hair —

"*Shh, chouja…*"

That was Renthor's voice, Brent realized. Indeed as soon as he registered the familiar nickname, his old acquaintance manifested in his mind's eye.

With the brim of his hat low over his face, Renthor put a finger to his smiling lips.

"*Keep your head down.*"

Like a dam exploding, the terror that Brent had just experienced ripped through him and he screamed. He screamed until he was sure his throat would tear open. Thrashing violently, he kicked and swung his arms about as if he'd gone mad.

"Stop!" he roared and his head spun as his body seemed to pivot, fighting against something that was holding him down. *"Let me go! No!"* He fought harder, writhing against whatever was gripping him, keeping him from escape.

It had him by the shoulders, his neck, his legs — he just couldn't break free —

"Brent —!" some distant voice shouted. But he could barely hear it above his own screaming.

"NO!"

He twisted free and a sharp pain seared his shoulder when he slammed into a hardwood surface. Something still had him around the legs and he kicked. He was nearly surprised when his foot slammed into something soft.

He didn't stop to wonder what it was but instead clawed out, only to crash into something else that was trying to bar his escape: a wall.

He yelled again, backing into it and kicking until the dark blanket that had entangled him was flung off. In the next instant someone drew close to him, seizing him by the shoulders as they shouted for him to be calm.

It was a woman's voice, and it was familiar.

Adelle?

No — it was…

"Calm *down,* Brent! It's all right!"

It was Xëri.

He clung to her, his fingers digging into her arms. His heart slammed in his chest and his yells lowered to gasps as he shuddered in her hold.

It wasn't until he'd reached that moment of calm was he able to recognize where he was: it was his new room in Chief Ivan's house.

There was a glass lantern a few feet away, lying on the ground, and to his right and pushed against the wall was his bed. The sheet and pillow were askew, and his blanket was in a heap on the floor.

"It's all right, Brent," Xëri soothed, stroking his back, and he crushed himself against her. "You're all right. I'm here. It's okay…it's okay…"

A sob blew through his pursed lips, and he buried his face in the warmth of her clothes.

Xëri held him, ignoring the severe pinching that was paining her arms as he clung to her, and her dark eyes shifted to the doorway.

Ivan was standing there, his body nearly taking up the entire frame. Peeking around one of his giant arms was Aaron.

Xëri fixed her eyes on the chief, and when she spoke her voice was low. "Ivan, he's *shaking.*"

Aaron's eyebrows rose and he tried to peek around his mother in order to see Brent's face. But all he could pick out was the boy's hunched form and spiky hair.

"Go back to your room, Aaron," Ivan said softly, pushing him back, and he emphasized the order in Katruskan, *"Itdi."*

Aaron glanced between him, his mother and Brent and then, with a face masked by reluctance and concern, he disappeared down the hall.

As he left, Ivan entered the room and knelt down next to Xëri. He put a hand on Brent's shoulder.

Brent lurched away from him with a shout and burrowed deeper into Xëri's arms, tightening his grip so much that she couldn't help but wince.

"Brent," Ivan called, spotting her pain, and he touched the boy again.

"Get away!" Brent shouted and he ripped away from Xëri only to slam into his bedside, his shoulders heaving.

Ivan pulled back and his eyebrows furrowed worriedly when the lantern caught Brent's red and crumpled face, along with the tears that were falling from his crinkled eyes.

"It was just a nightmare, Brent," Xëri promised him, touching his shoulder. When he flinched and threw his eyes at her, she drew back. "You're safe. This is Taranis, remember? You're safe here. Everything's okay."

"T...Taranis?" Brent echoed weakly and Xëri nodded.

"What do you need, Brent?" Ivan asked as the boy stared into space, his rapid breathing finally beginning to slow.

"I..." Brent's eyes were still glazed over. He looked exhausted.

"I…I need…to see Adelle."

Xëri's eyebrows arched despairingly and she shared a hesitant glance with her husband. "Brent," she started but unsure of how to go on, she fell silent.

"Please…" One last tear escaped Brent's eye, perfectly caught by the flickering firelight in the lantern. "I want…to see her…" His body slowly sagged and his eyelids drooped. "Please…"

Xëri watched him and the crease in her forehead deepened as her sorrow mounted. "…Brent, Adelle isn't —"

"I know," he croaked.

It wasn't a dream.

Xëri volunteered to take Brent to Adelle's grave. She also suggested that just the two of them go. Going along with anyone else would probably overwhelm him, she said.

He'd been grateful for that.

By the time they reached Adelle's grave, his eyes had dried and the racing of his heart had ebbed. With his face unreadable he stared at her headstone, Xëri a few yards behind him, and he barely shivered when an early morning wind rushed over the hill.

Several petals broke free of the amari tree to dance in that wind, shifting his hair and clothes with it, and when it finally passed he parted his lips and raised his eyes to the hilly horizon.

His voice was quiet. "Adelle didn't blame me…when she died."

With her pointy ears prickling at the sound of his voice, Xëri drew herself out of her dreary thoughts and fixed her eyes on him.

"Do you think she would've lived, if I hadn't met her?" Brent turned to look at her and by the soft pink of dawn's light, Xëri saw that new tears had fallen from his eyes.

She paused and then stepped forward. "…The truth is, no one lives forever, Brent," she replied and when she came up beside him, she gazed at the grave solemnly.

Brent didn't respond. He just followed her line of sight with his own.

"Adelle was always putting the needs of others before her own," Xëri added. "That was who she was. She was like family to everyone."

"...I'm sorry."

Xëri's eyes moved from Adelle's grave to Brent, her eyebrows having risen at the way his voice had broken with emotion. By the time she viewed him, he was wiping his face with the heels of his hands.

"I...never meant to hurt her..." Brent sniffed and with a soft smile, Xëri placed a comforting hand on his shoulder.

"If I knew anything about Adelle, it's that she was always aware of what she was doing," she told him. "She put herself in danger every day, helping Avats. She even helped me once. Years ago.

"But that was what she loved to do. She loved to help people. And Brent..." Smiling warmly, she waited until he looked up at her. "She loved helping you. She cared for you very, very much. And she wanted you to be happy. I can promise you that."

"But...why?" Brent's eyebrows crinkled with confusion. "If she knew she was gonna get in trouble...why would she help me?"

He suddenly thought of Aaron, and of how he wanted to become a raider. Why would anyone want to put themselves in danger for someone else?

Xëri's eyes moved to the side thoughtfully and then she lifted her chin so that she could look at the horizon. As the gentle rays of light bled over the mountaintops to strike the valley below, she spoke again.

"There are a lot of dangers in this world," she began, turning from the light, "and often, people don't want to do anything that will get them caught up in those dangers. But Adelle didn't care for that. And that was because she believed that there were more important things than her own safety."

Brent stared at her and then he looked down at Adelle's headstone again. "So then...she thought my safety was more important than hers?"

Xëri nodded and passed him a soft smile. "Yes. Yours, mine, and everyone else she's ever helped."

Brent fell silent and with his eyes dropping to his feet, he sniffed. "I wish…I wish I could've saved her instead."

Xëri's eyes glistened sadly. "Brent…"

"Then she'd still be here…" His vision blurred and he swallowed roughly.

Xëri's forehead creased and she fell to her knees beside him. After placing a hand on one of his shoulders she cupped his cheek with the other, urging him to look at her. When his moist gaze found hers, she held it emphatically.

"Brent. Don't ever wish yourself away," she ordered. "If you'd been hurt instead, Adelle would've never forgiven herself. You're here now, Brent. You're alive, and you're *free*. And I know that that alone would make her happy.

"So you can't wish yourself away," her hand fell from his face to grip his other shoulder. "Because your life, the fact that you could exist even if she couldn't, made her glad."

Brent pressed his lips together, holding in his cries, and he forced a brisk nod.

"So live, Brent." Xëri's hands slid down to his and she held them tightly. "Live, because life has been given to you."

He nodded again, quicker this time, and when Xëri opened her arms he dropped into her embrace, cushioned by her hold as the light of morning beamed around them.

22

O KAY..." WITH CHILDREN both older and younger than him cheering at his back, Aaron gripped the handle of the tonfa that was strapped to his right hip. Slipping it out of its holster he twirled it outwards, then flipped it back against his forearm.

Bending his knees, he flicked his bright blue eyes between the two people that were standing opposite him. "Ready?"

"Ready." Liam, who was standing diagonally to his left, bent into his own stance. He was also carrying a wooden weapon, but instead of a tonfa it was a curved, single-edged sword.

"Same here!" Renée announced from opposite him, her pose being one of bended knees and spread feet. She also carried a practice sword but it was thin, straight and double-edged. Her hair was tied up with a white bird feather that was attached to a beaded string, and resolution shone in her dark eyes.

"Go, Ren!" Mekial cheered from within the crowd.

It was close to midmorning, or just past, and the summer sun bore down on them with rising heat as noon approached.

But neither Aaron, Liam, Renée, nor any of the boys and girls surrounding them were bothered by it. They were used to this weather. The breezes that rolled over the distant hills and into the village did well to keep them cool, too.

But at the same time the wind was a little annoying, because they were all gathered on a large patch of dirt that stretched out along Taranis' western side. Every now and then, the wind would cause some of the soil to spiral around their legs or swirl about their eyes.

But they were used to that too, because this dirt field was a place that they often came to.

The schoolhouse was here and so was the sparring hall, the latter of which was built just in front of the forest that walled Taranis' northern end. Both buildings were popular for Aaron, Liam and Renée, because the schoolhouse was where they learned, and the sparring hall was where they trained.

After all, Aaron wasn't the only one who wanted to be a raider.

"All right-y!" Eklaire skipped out of the crowd and into the center of the triangle that her friends had formed. Her short, stark-white hair bounced as she moved and it swung about as she spiraled to look at everyone. "I'll go ahead'n count off!" As she spoke, she extended an object that she was holding in her hands.

At first glance it looked like a ball, but a closer look proved that it was more than that: covered in a thick outer coat of dried grass that had been tied together, it was more of a handmade weight, with a filling of mud that was sealed beneath layers of roped up animal hide.

Evidently different from the average ball, which was typically made of dried animal skin and any kind of soft filling that the children could get their hands on, this ball was used for a more sober purpose — one that Aaron, Liam and Renée were bent on exploiting.

"On three!" Eklaire looked at the trio and they dug their heels into the ground. "One!" she shouted and the other children joined in. "Two…!"

Lowering the ball and bending her knees she paused for dramatic effect, her mismatched eyes dancing.

Some of the children laughed or bristled with suspense, and they nearly jumped when Eklaire at last cried, *"Three!"*

Swinging her arms, she tossed the weighted sphere up in Aaron's direction.

At the same time, the children unleashed a mighty, two-worded cheer: *"Mud Baaaall!"* [tv]

MUD BALL!
CODE: GIVEITYOURALL

Their voices carried into the village, startling some while others glanced up with a knowing smile.

Only in one place did their yell happen to stir a sleeping villager, ringing in his pointed ears and making him groan.

Brent rolled onto his back and then went still, knitting his brow beneath the sunbeams that flowed in through his window. He moaned again.

But his ears continued to hone in on the sound of distant shouting.

He screwed his eyes up crossly. Then he got up and stumbled into the hallway.

Running a hand along the wall, he followed the short corridor to the foyer and cast his eyes to the left. The dining room was there, set with a square wooden table, four matching chairs, and tasseled tapestries that hung next to the window.

Fixing his eyes on the table, he saw a small bowl sitting on it. It was filled with berries.

Without a second's thought he took some. At the same time he turned to see the room that was opposite him.

It was the kitchen, with a wooden sink, a large basin of water, dish shelves, cabinets, and a pot oven. The entire area looked clean. He guessed that Xëri had tidied it up recently.

On that note he shifted his gaze once more, this time to the small, second-floor balcony that jutted over the end of the hallway. Training his ears to that level of the house, he deduced that neither Ivan nor Xëri were home.

He was used to their not being around when he woke up by now. On his first day it'd troubled him, but Aaron had calmed him and told him that in the mornings, his parents left to attend to their village duties. They were usually gone by the time he himself woke up.

At the thought of Aaron, Brent wondered where he was. He was usually still around when Brent awoke.

No sooner had that thought crossed his mind did a fresh cheer sound from the depths of the village.

Popping another berry into his mouth, he made his way to the door. Halfway there he stopped, backtracked to the bowl of berries, and took some more.

Outside, he was greeted by a warm wind that whisked through his hair. Eating another berry he started down the path in front of him, which inclined towards the Main House.

Some other villagers were scattered along the path, too, following it to their own destinations. Without a hint of fear for his exposed ears, Brent walked among them.

He barely paid them any attention. Only when they greeted him did he look up and return their calls with a soft smile or a wave.

In his short time in Taranis he'd learned that the villagers were rather friendly, and as the blue-haired child that had been adopted by their chief they'd come to recognize him fairly easily.

Their kindness had been strange to him at first, frightening even. But after seeing that they harbored no deceitful intent, he got used to it.

"Good morning, Brent," an elderly woman said as he walked past.

He swallowed another berry. "Morning, Greta."

The old woman's little eyes crinkled with a brightening of her smile.

Brent didn't know much about her, only that she was one of the women who sewed clothes for the villagers. She was short and a little hunchbacked, with white hair that was tied into a high bun, revealing her round ears. A burgundy dress hemmed with olive green emblems was her selected outfit, and over her shoulders was a beautifully decorated shawl. Her feathered necklaces complemented it nicely.

He wasn't sure if she'd been the one to create the outfit that he wore now. But he did know that she'd been the one to give him the beaded jade necklace that currently hung about his neck.

He'd been grateful for it. It made him feel like one of the villagers.

After all, jade jewelry — whether it was in the form of a necklace, bracelet, hairpiece or anklet — was an accessory that everyone seemed to have.

"Are you headed to the field by the schoolhouse?" she asked

him.

He looked at her curiously.

"All the other boys and girls are down there, making a wild noise," she explained. "I think they're playing a game of some kind."

"I'll go see," Brent said and he made to hasten off towards the schoolhouse.

"If you see Liam down there, tell him I've got those garments for his sister ready," she called after him, and he stopped. "She's far too tired to go anywhere these days. He needs to help the poor girl out a little."

"Okay!" Brent nodded and turned tail again, jogging down the rest of the path and turning onto the main road.

He skirted around some more villagers as he followed it, returning their greetings as he did. Reaching the bridge that arched over the stream he crossed it, and on the other side he hurried down a narrow road.

All the while the children's voices echoed around him, filling his ears with the muffled cry of, *"Mud Baaaall!"*

He frowned.

A second later he stepped out onto the dirt field. There, he spotted a crowd of boys and girls surrounding Aaron, Liam and Renée.

No sooner had he noticed them were his eyes drawn to the grassy ball that was arching up and down between them, batted skyward by their wooden weapons.

Eating the last of his berries, he went to the edge of the small gathering. Seeing Eklaire on the inner part of it, he weaved his way towards her.

"Mud Ball! Mud Ball!" she was crying when he reached her.

"What's 'Mud Ball'?" he asked and his frown returned.

Eklaire glanced back at him and did a double-take. "Oh, hey-a, Brent! What a surprise seein' you here!"

"Hi, Brent!" Renée shouted, spotting his bright blue hair.

"Don't get distracted by your boyfriend, Ren! Or else you'll have to clean the whole — classroom!" Aaron said, hitting the ball over to her as he finished his sentence.

"He's not my boyfriend!" Renée hit the ball back to him. "And I am *not* cleaning the classroom!"

Aaron sniggered. "Says you!" Spinning his tonfa, he hit the ball back to her.

It broke open enough for thick droplets of mud to shoot out and splatter the ground.

"Is that ball full of mud?" Brent observed, his eyebrows rising.

"That's the point!" Eklaire rounded on him spiritedly. "Mud Ball's when you go ahead'n whack that ball at the other people! And if it breaks on ya, you lose!"

Brent looked at the ball just as it fell towards Renée.

"Got it!" she cried, the children yelling behind her, and she adjusted the hold on her sword. She swung it — hard — knocking it over to Liam and freeing a few speckles of mud.

He smacked it back to her.

"It's gonna break!" she cried, hitting it to Aaron.

"Mud Ball! Mud Ball!" Eklaire chanted again, her blue and green eyes glittering.

"Not on me!" Aaron denied, twirling his tonfa and, controlling his strength, he knocked it to Liam.

"C'mon, Mud Ball!" Eklaire whined.

Liam hit the ball towards Renée. "You might have to wait a little longer, Eklaire," he called.

Renée smacked the ball to Aaron.

"Not too much longer, it's gonna break soon!" Aaron shouted, hitting it back to her. "My arkans are on Ren! Get ready to clean the classroom!"

"Hey!" Renée frowned and hit the ball back to him.

He knocked it towards Liam again, and this time a little bit of mud mixed with grass flew out. "It's gonna break!" he warned, echoing Renée's words.

"Mud Ball! Mud Ball!" Eklaire started up again.

The children joined her, clapping their hands or jumping up and down in excitement.

Again, Liam smacked the ball in Renée's direction.

She readied herself, spreading her feet and digging her heels into the dirt. When the ball was in reach she swung her sword out and…!

PHLAAPP!

The ball broke against it, unleashing a mighty explosion of mud and grass that doused her until she was covered from head to toe with grassy, wet dirt. Even a layer of animal hide slapped atop her head.

Dropping her sword she yelled in surprise, her eyes scrunched and arms flying up in protection.

Behind her some of the children jumped back, laughing or gawking at the fact that Renée really had been the one to get mud-ball'd.

Across the triangle, Liam chuckled.

Aaron grinned. "Looks like you *are* cleaning up the classroom this month!" He loosened his stance.

"Ugh…" After wiping the mud off her face, Renée flung it off of her hands with a flick of her wrists. She turned when a particular giggle came from behind her.

"Mom's gonna be mad!" Mekial was laughing.

Renée glared at him, mud dripping from her chin. But then her own face split into a mischievous grin. "Yeah — at both of us!"

Before Mekial could even think to run away, she scooped him into a muddy embrace.

"Eww! Ahh! No, lemme go!" The boy squirmed in her arms. "You're all muddy!"

"But I just love you so much!" Renée cried. A split second later she lost her hold on him, because he became just as slippery as she was.

With a grunt he dropped to his feet, staggering as he tried to wipe the dirt off of his front.

Around him, the children made him the new target of their laughter.

He frowned at first. Then he spread his arms wide. "You want some?!" He grabbed mud off his chest and threw it at them, causing much giggling and surprised yells of, "Hey!"

"Why were you guys playing with a ball of mud?" Brent asked, approaching the triangle that Aaron, Liam and Renée were still standing in.

"It's a training game," Aaron said. "Jeffrey says it's s'posed to help us with muscle control."

Brent's frown was so potent that it was as if he thought Aaron had spoken another language.

Liam noticed. "Jeffrey is the one who trains us," he explained as he walked over to where Brent and Aaron were standing. "Over there." He pointed at the rectangular, one-story building that was the sparring hall.

Brent looked at it. "He trains you? For what?"

"So we can use these!" Aaron held up his tonfa.

Brent eyed it inquisitively. "What *is* that?"

"It's called a tonfa." Aaron looked at it admiringly. "It's the weapon I wanna use when I finally become an auction raider. I only use one now but when I get better, I'll be able to use two of 'em at the same time! Maybe I'll even get to use the ones with the blades hidden inside!"

"And that's the weapon you're using?" Brent asked, switching his gaze to Liam and dropping it to his sword.

Liam barely glanced at it. "Yeah."

"So," Brent's eyebrows creased, "you *both* want to become raiders?"

"Yeah," Liam said again, nodding.

Aaron did the same.

"Renée, too?" Brent looked at her to find that she was still playing with Mekial and the other children, ducking beneath the clumps of mud that they were throwing at each other or forcing muddy hugs onto them.

Eklaire had joined in the fray, too. Her white hair and clothes were already stained with clods of mud.

"Ren, too," Liam affirmed, following Brent's eyes.

Brent paused for a second and his eyes fell in a fleeting moment of thought.

He looked at Aaron and Liam again. "Why?"

"What do you mean, why?" Aaron asked, his expression one of offense.

"Well…" Brent hesitated, somewhat taken aback by how quickly, and even, how unfavorably Aaron had reacted. "You're…not afraid of getting caught?"

At that, Aaron's frown collapsed into bafflement. "What for?"

"Don't people get hurt, going out on raids?" Brent went on and even as he asked, he recalled the last raiding mission that he'd heard of.

Only a few days after he'd been brought to Taranis, he'd seen a team of villagers go out again, some of their faces familiar to him while others were harder to place. Where they'd gone he hadn't known, but he did know that while walking past the stream a couple of days later, he'd overheard some villagers saying that several members of that team either hadn't returned or had been severely injured.

"Why would you wanna do that?" he asked. "What if you don't come back?"

Aaron's frown returned, but this time it was one of pensive contemplation instead of offense. He'd never considered Brent's thought before.

"Someone has to help those people," he said finally and his once distant eyes were full of purpose. "No one should have to go through what they go through. Some of these guys have even lost their families to slavery. And some of them used to be slaves themselves." He looked at the children that Renée and Eklaire were playing with.

Brent looked with him.

"And it's not fair."

Brent's eyes jumped back to Aaron.

"That's why I wanna be a raider," he finished. "And every time I get to go out on a raid, I'll make sure to avenge them." His face hardened. "Slave traders don't deserve sympathy for what they do."

Brent's eyebrows furrowed nervously. The growl in Aaron's voice was unnerving.

Liam was quiet.

"That's why I helped you, y'know," Aaron added, his scowl leaving him. "You needed someone. Plus, you were almost gonna get trampled by all those people."

Brent blinked, surprised, embarassed, and yet grateful all at once.

"You're lucky he was there," Liam said plainly. "We're still trainees; we're not supposed to go out on msisions yet."

"R-right!" Aaron exclaimed, realizing, and he turned on Brent. "So don't tell my dad I was out in Peluma! I could get in huge trouble!" He calmed shortly after this confession, considering something. "But why were *you* out there? Were you a slave, too? Did you run away from your master or something?"

"Oh…" Brent glanced away. "I, um…"

Aaron cocked his head with a dubious squint of his eye.

"Something like that, I guess…"

"Hmm." Aaron seemed accepting of his answer. "I think you should join, Brent." With a fanciful twirl of his tonfa, he stuffed it into his holster. "You'd probably be good."

"With trainin'?" Eklaire hopped into their circle. Mud was smeared all over her shirt, face and hair. Looking between them, her eyes stopped on Brent. "Yer gonna train with 'em?"

"I, uh…" Brent faltered. "Um…"

"Brent's gonna train with us?" Renée burst excitedly, stopping herself right before she hurled another pile of mud at one of the children.

"I don't think he's sure yet," Liam said, having thrown an intuitive glance in Brent's direction.

"But if you did, all of us'd be able to hang out!" Renée dropped her mud and came towards the group.

Behind her, Mekial and the other children continued to throw mud at each other, laughing hysterically.

"Do you train with them too, Eklaire?" Brent asked, looking at her.

"Naw, not me!" She giggled and rubbed the back of her head in an uncommonly shy way. "I may not look it, but I actually get sick a lot. I'd just slow ya'll down."

"I'll say," Aaron sighed. "She gets sick at the weirdest times! In the middle of summer, whenever we go to the lake —"

"I didn't get sick last time we went to the lake!" she protested. "And that was yesterday!"

"You were sneezing and blowing your nose for the rest of the day," Liam reminded her.

"And you get sick in the fall and spring…" Aaron rattled on.

"Not all the time…!" Eklaire made to argue again but she suddenly interrupted herself with a surge of coughing that forced her to duck away, her hands over her mouth.

"And when she gets worked up," Aaron finished.

Eklaire straightened up, struggling to catch her breath.

Brent looked at her worriedly. "Are you okay?"

"Yeah…I'm okay." Eklaire faced him with a tired smile.

"It looks like you're still not over your cold, yet," Liam observed, his face one of subtle concern.

"She'll be fine." Aaron waved a hand. "Anyway Brent, there's no training today cuz Jeffrey's still off on a mission. But there's gonna be training tomorrow, cuz he's s'posed to be back tonight."

"Oh." Brent shrank back a little, unsure as to how else he should respond to that. After all, it wasn't like he wanted to be a raider.

Aaron studied him quietly and soon registered his soft tone as one of hushed reluctance. "Well," he raised a shoulder, "I guess you can just think about it."

"Yeah, no worries!" Eklaire assured him. "Not everyone's a raider, but by the time everybody's all grown up they find their own way of helpin' out 'round the village! Some people build houses, or go huntin', or make clothes, or cook for the new villagers, or work in the schoolhouse, or make weapons, or make cool doohickeys for the raiders…"

"You've pretty much got a lot of options," Aaron concluded, having noticed Brent's dumbfounded look.

"So the choice is all yours!" Eklaire exclaimed. "But if you wanna hang out with these fellas, you'd hafta be an auction raider, too. The raiders're usually real busy, cuz they got all sorts of things to do."

Brent blinked curiously. "Like what?"

"She said most of 'em," Aaron said. "There's the main job of auction raiding. Some of the raiders join hunting parties too. Or, if any of our supporters send word that they've got slaves with them, the raiders meet them in the Empire and smuggle the slaves back here. They also do recon."

"What's recon?"

"It's reconnaissance," Renée answered. "It's when scouts study a possible raiding site and then they tell the raiders here what it looks like. That's what my dad does when he doesn't have a raiding assignment. But some scouts stay in the Empire and send word to Taranis about upcoming slave auctions for us to raid."

Brent's eyebrows went up and then dove into creases that rippled between his eyes. "Wait…how does anyone send word to Taranis without any imperials finding out?"

"With the Lyrikan magpies!" Eklaire cheered, tossing her arms into the air energetically. "They're these real smart birds that can take a message to anyone almost anywhere in the whole Empire! But I hear since they're so common in the province out yonder, the scouts use 'em to send messages 'round here."

"So the imperials never notice 'em," Aaron concluded, his arms crossing with a proud look in his eye.

"There are also villagers who handle border control," Liam put in.

Brent scrunched an eyebrow at that. "Border control?"

"Yeah. You saw the wall in front of the valley, right?" Aaron asked.

The folds in Brent's forehead deepened. "Wall?"

"You didn't see it when you first came here?" Aaron quirked an eyebrow but didn't push him about it. "Well, there's this giant wall of trees and super thick vines and stuff that hides this whole valley from Odelwhite Forest, so the Empire can't find us. Some of the walls are also placed in gaps in the mountain ranges, too. Only an aetheriest can open the way through them. But sometimes, we find out that soldiers are poking around near them in search of new territory to explore. My Dad has border control scouts go out there to get rid of 'em. They're all aetheriests."

"How do they get rid of the soldiers?" Brent asked.

"They try not to be too obvious, otherwise the imperials'll figure out we're here," Aaron said. "So they just create illusions. You know, scary animals, or making a part of the forest denser than it really is so they get turned around…that sorta stuff.

"But it's not always that cool, cuz we don't have to deal with threats like those a whole lot." Aaron actually looked disappointed. "Like, I heard there was this landslide a couple months ago and the border scouts went to gauge the damage and see if the wall that was there needed fixing. It sounded like a pretty boring mission overall."

"Ooh, I remember that!" Eklaire exclaimed. "That was when we had all them nasty thunderstorms!"

"Yeah, and you got sick. As usual."

"It wasn't my fault!"

Brent paused to absorb all the information he'd been given.

If every villager did have to contribute to the community, he was grateful that becoming an auction raider wasn't his only option. There wasn't a fiber in his being that wanted to lay eyes on the Empire again.

But for some reason, he felt guilty about that.

He wondered if it was because the closest friends that he'd ever had were standing in front of him, saying that they wanted to go into the Empire and rescue the people that were in chains, bound to masters who'd separated their families and stolen their rights to freedom.

Eklaire's reason for rejecting the plan was health-related. But Brent was sure that if she wasn't so frail, she'd probably join them.

Was it fair then, for him to reject being a raider simply because he didn't want to go back into the Empire?

Aaron used his hate for the place as motivation. So was it right for Brent to use his as a reason to stay away?

He didn't know. But there was one thing that he knew for certain: the way his friends placed the safety of others above their own reminded him of Adelle.

At that, he wondered if he *should* take up auction raiding. Maybe if he did, he'd feel worthy of Adelle's sacrifice.

But if he became a raider, wasn't there a chance that he would die like she did?

Already he could imagine it: his body toppling backward, punctured by an arrow that freed his life's blood to spill around him.

His heart rolled like thunder in his ears.

Maybe he wouldn't do it after all.

"Brent?" Renée leaned forward and cocked her head to the side. Something shimmered in his lost gaze, she noticed, something vulnerable and tender. Her eyebrows puckered. "Are you okay…?"

"Yeah." He returned to the present and if only for a moment, he forced his frightening thoughts away. He didn't want to become a raider.

But he didn't want his friends to think any less of him, either.

"And, um…maybe…" He didn't look at her. "I'll think about being a raider."

"So you wanna do it?" Renée asked and her face lit up just a little.

Brent pursed his lips bracingly. "I'll just…think about it," he said haltingly and with a drop of his heart he noticed a glint of disappointment shoot through her eyes.

"Okay…"

"Aw, cheer up, Ren. It's not like he has to figure it out today, anyway." Aaron dropped his hand onto his tonfa. "Anyway, I say we play another round of Mud Ball! This time, the loser's gotta do everyone's chores for a month! My arkans are on Ren!"

"Hey!" Renée glared at him. "I'm already stuck cleaning the classroom for a month! You're just getting big-headed cuz you won!"

"Oh, am I?" Aaron smiled slyly, his arms folding. "Or are you just chickening out?"

Renée gasped, offended. "You're on!"

"I actually think Aaron'll lose this time," Liam theorized.

"What?" Aaron frowned. "Why?"

"Because if you keep challenging Ren, she'll eventually show you up," he said. "Remember the last time you taunted her during sparring?"

"Ooh-hoo, boy!" Eklaire grinned. "You sure got yer behind beat that day, Aaron!"

"Yeah! So get ready to do my chores!" Renée pointed at him.

"Ha! We'll see about that!" Aaron returned her fiery glare of determination.

"Should this be a one-on-one then?" Eklaire asked, looking between them.

"No." Liam faced Aaron. "I want Aaron to do my chores, too."

"You're siding against me?!" Aaron rounded on him, shocked.

Liam's matter-of-fact look was steadfast. "Yep."

"Liam!"

"Then get ready to do all of our chores, Aaron!" Renée proclaimed and her dark eyes turned to her brother and the other children. "Hey, guys! You wanna watch us beat Aaron at Mud Ball?!"

"I'll go get the other ball!" Eklaire announced as the children cheered excitedly, their mud-splattered faces beaming.

"Brent, you wanna watch, too?" Renée faced him as Eklaire jogged towards one of the nearby houses. One more Mud Ball was leaning against it.

Brent looked at Renée. With a slight drop of his chin, he decided that he'd watch.

Renée nodded back and rounded on the others, her face alight as she went to join them.

So it was that with her back turned, she didn't see the troubled shadow that passed over his face, shading his eyes as his brow furrowed anxiously.

23

AARON LOST, JUST like Liam predicted.

Dropping his tonfa he released a loud yell when the Mud Ball broke over him, covering him in a shameful mess of mud, grass and animal hide.

Growling, he glared at his mud-caked limbs. Then with a heavy sigh, he asked for the chores he was now doomed to carry out.

But he was spared.

Some of the children's mothers arrived at that point, saying that it was time for the little ones to come home for lunch. But when they saw how muddy they all were, they demanded that they clean up first. Aaron, Renée and Eklaire were told to do the same.

"The Luminoro Watch is tonight!" they reminded them. "You don't want to be all dirty for that."

When Brent asked what they were talking about, he didn't get a straight answer. He was only told that he'd find out that night.

Raising his eyebrows, he was filled with an incurable eagerness for the dark of day to come.

The children, along with Aaron, Eklaire and Renée, left their muddy playground and followed the mothers down to the river.

Brent and Liam were the only ones who weren't in need of any cleaning. So instead of going to the river, they decided to go back to Taranis.

They went in a silence that Brent hated.

Even though the distant chirping of birds, whispers of the wind and the sound of villagers talking kept the air from being eerily quiet, he felt awkward.

"Um." The sound left him before he could stop it.

Liam didn't say anything.

Brent assumed that he hadn't heard him. But when he remembered that Liam's hearing was better than his own, he changed that thought: he was being ignored.

He frowned. But he still decided to say something else. "What're you gonna do now?"

"I think I have to get water for my sister," Liam answered, his brow suddenly furrowing with thought. "She probably used all the water that we have."

"Why'd she do that?"

Liam shrugged. "I don't really get it, but she likes when I boil it. She says that the steam helps her relax."

Brent couldn't see the connection. "Why does she need help relaxing?"

"I think it's cuz she's really pregnant. At least, that's what the other moms say."

Brent still didn't understand. "What does that mean?"

Liam looked at him as they neared the village stream. "What does what mean?"

"Pregnant."

"What —?!" Liam's usually blank face actually cracked into one of surprise. "You don't know what it means for someone to be pregnant? And why do you look just as surprised as I am?"

Brent blinked soundlessly, his eyebrows still raised and eyes still wide. "Because I've never seen *you* look surprised! Is it that bad that I don't know what 'pregnant' is?"

"It..." Liam's astonishment melted into a thoughtful frown as he turned away, one hand masking the lower half of his face. "Hm...it's when...oh."

He stopped, his eyes now fixed on something ahead, and Brent slowed to a halt next to him.

Liam pointed at what had snagged his attention. "See that woman right there?"

Brent followed his finger and soon spotted who Liam was

talking about.

On the other side of the stream there was a group of women who were talking together. The one Liam was pointing out was the shortest, with thick, curly black hair and calm, brown eyes that matched her dark skin.

She was skinny, but her size didn't match her big stomach. She had a hand resting on it and at something one of her friends said, she laughed and rubbed it tenderly.

Liam dropped his hand. "That's pregnant."

"Oh."

So that was it.

If that was the case then he'd seen plenty of pregnant women back in the city. He simply hadn't known what the proper term for them was.

In fact, he didn't even know why they had such big stomachs in the first place.

"Did she eat too much?" His eyes shot to Liam when the boy actually stifled a laugh.

"No." The smile was still apparent on his lips. "There's a baby in her belly."

"Oh." Brent looked at the woman again. It reminded him of something. "By the way, Greta said that she had something for your sister." He looked at Liam. "Garments, I think."

Liam's eyes lit with understanding. "Oh. The baby's clothes."

"The baby?" Brent pointed at the woman while looking at him. "*That* kind of baby? How would it wear clothes?"

Liam frowned. "When it comes out."

Brent's brow pursed. "It's gonna come out?"

"Yeah."

"How?"

Liam's cheeks turned pink. "I think you should ask someone else that question."

"Huh…like Ivan?"

"Yeah…" The flush in Liam's face faded. "Maybe. Anyway, I'll go and see Greta. See you later." He started off, but before he could get too far Brent reached out and snatched his arm.

"Wait!" he blurted and Liam peered back at him, his familiar, unreadable expression having returned. "I...I wanted to ask you one more thing."

Liam looked reluctant. "It's not about how babies are made, is it?"

Brent shook his head.

Liam slipped out of his hold and faced him. "Then what is it?"

"Why do you want to be a raider?"

As with most of Liam's responses, his answer was a direct one. "So other Avats can find a home."

Brent's shoulders loosened and his stare became incredulous.

"I want to help them find a home," Liam elaborated. "Taranis became my home a few months ago, and I like it here. I want it to be a home for other Avats, too."

"You're not scared of dying?" Brent asked next, his brow creasing.

Liam stared at him. "Dying?"

"Helping Avats...it might get you in big trouble. And you could die for it." Brent raised his shoulders tensely. "You're not scared?"

Liam didn't immediately answer. But when he did, his voice was even. "I guess I would be scared. But I've almost died plenty of times before. So I don't think about it. I just make sure I don't die."

Brent's surprise was blatant.

Liam slanted his body away, indicating that he was about to leave. "I have to go and get that stuff for my sister. I'll see you." He took one step away. But then he turned back. "Oh — so does this mean you decided to come to training tomorrow?"

Brent held his gaze for a second. Then he lowered his eyes shamefully. "I don't know yet."

Liam eyed his downcast face. "You can just watch, like Eklaire does," he pointed out.

Brent raised his eyes.

"You don't have to become a raider if you don't want to."

Brent didn't respond.

"Well...see you." Liam turned and walked up the hill.

Brent stared after him, his brow slightly furrowed, and it was in pensive silence that he cast his eyes to the side once more.

24

FOR ALMOST THE rest of the day, Brent found himself wondering a lot about Liam and his view of death. For instance, how had Liam faced it, and what had made it so he didn't think of it anymore? How could anyone so young face death and yet harbor no ill feelings towards it? Who had tried to kill him? Why had they wanted to kill him?

He wanted to know the answer to all of those questions and more, but he wasn't sure how to go about finding them. He supposed he could ask Liam directly, but he didn't think that that would be appropriate. After all Liam seemed unapproachable now, as if his apathy towards death suddenly made him too great to be associated with.

In the end, Brent could only wonder. So, he decided to discard the thoughts completely.

He couldn't satisfy them anyway, and even if he did pester Liam he doubted it'd help. He probably wouldn't be keen on illustrating his past, especially given the fact that he'd glazed over his having various, near-death experiences.

So, Brent took to focusing on his chores instead, all of which ranged from helping to skin or pluck the animals that the hunting party had returned with to cleaning his room.

He was also recruited to accompany a gathering party into the woods, with whom he collected nuts, fruits and herbs for the entire village. When he finished, he was even allowed to snack on a few berries as a reward for his participation.

These tasks and more were charged to him, and it was only for a small handful of them that he wound up working with one of his friends.

The only one he never partnered with was Liam. In fact he only crossed paths with him once and bearing his typical, emotionless expression, Liam didn't seem to notice him at all.

Or maybe he did.

Brent wasn't sure.

But instead of linger on the possibility of it he went about the rest of his day as if the brief passing had never occurred.

So, he became wholly absorbed in the duties that were placed before him, and his sense of time was lost until he later looked out of a window and saw that the sky was blazing with the scorching hues of sunset. Not too soon after making this discovery he was dismissed from his final task, which had been a menial charge of scrubbing the tables in the Main House's dining hall.

At first, with nothing left to occupy himself with, he was at a loss as to what he should do for the rest of the day.

But he didn't have to wonder for long, because as soon as he left the Main House he saw that activity within Taranis had increased.

Everywhere villagers were walking along the main road and from his vantage point atop the Main House's porch, he saw that they were grouping at its base.

Peering through the setting sun's glaring rays, he spotted some of the children darting around the older villagers as they headed for the same place.

One of the adults that they scurried around he swiftly recognized and after hurrying down the steps of the Main House's outer deck, he made his way towards her.

"Greta!" he called and when her small eyes found him, they crinkled with a friendly smile. "What's going on? Where's everybody going?"

"To the Luminoro Watch," she responded as he stopped in front of her. "Around this time of year we all gather at the edge of the village and go to see it together. Didn't you hear?"

All at once, Brent remembered how he'd first heard of the event only earlier that day. Again his mouth opened, this time to ask what the Watch actually was, but before he could he heard his name being shouted.

Turning from Greta, he looked at a side road that opened up beside the Main House. From there Eklaire was running to him, waving a beaded arm as she jogged out of the path's shadows.

As always, her face was bright. But Brent also saw that her cheeks were a little flushed.

He wondered how long she'd been running.

"I've been lookin' for ya all over!" she cried as she neared him, her arm falling, and without stopping or giving him a chance to respond, she grabbed his hand. "C'mon!"

He barely grunted before she yanked him away from Greta so as to half-lead, half-pull him down the hill.

Regaining his balance so that he wouldn't trip and fall, he looked up and saw that the many who'd already amassed at the bottom of the road were talking in pairs or groups as they waited for the rest of the village. Several he recognized only by their faces, but after a hasty scan of the entire assembly he saw that there were some he also knew by name.

Isabel and Richter were the first that he spotted, both of them standing apart because they were engaged in separate conversations. Renée and Mekial's parents were there, too.

There was even someone with Liam, which Brent figured out because he was talking to that particular person away from his friends. Judging by her round belly and how her facial features were similar to his, Brent was left to assume that she was his older sister.

He'd never seen her before and upon remembering how both Greta and Liam had implied her pregnancy to be straining her body, he figured that that was why.

She was much younger than he'd thought, close to her late teens at best, and she had a head of long and thick black hair that was styled into a high ponytail. It was then that he realized she was a Southern Avat.

He wondered why she didn't have albinism like her brother. Was it not a family trait?

He had no way of knowing. In any case, when he saw her hand

resting on her stomach, he saw that she was indeed "really pregnant".

Unlike with her, Renée and Mekial's parents he had met, and he liked them as much as he did Ivan and Xëri.

Ben was their father, a tan-skinned man with broad shoulders and big biceps, as well as a height that was a few inches shy of six feet. His hair was also black, short and somewhat spiky. On one occasion Brent had asked how he made it stand up that way and in response, Ben had explained that it was thanks to a paste he created with the help of several plant oils.

"Maybe I'll show you how to make it sometime," he'd offered, and Brent had liked the sound of that.

Terra, their mother, was slim and fit, with boyishly short black hair, brown skin and dark eyes that had been passed down to her children.

Like her husband she was a raider and she had a naturally serious demeanor about her character, which complemented her spouse's more lenient and fun-loving personality. She could also be intimidating in a way reminiscent of Mrs. Scott but at the same time, Brent never sensed any hostility from her.

Ivan and Xëri were the only ones that he couldn't find, in spite of how Aaron was present. He didn't need to speculate why though, because he'd seen them at the Main House when he'd left it.

What he did want to know was whether or not they'd be joining him and what appeared to be most of the village in observing this "Luminoro Watch".

He didn't have to wait long for an answer.

"I found him!" Eklaire shouted as she pulled him into their circle of friends. "We're ready to go!"

"It is going to start soon," Terra said and beside her Ben swooped Mekial off his feet, making him laugh. "We should start heading off, before we miss it."

"Wait, now?" Brent looked from her to the others as Eklaire released his hand. "But, what about everyone at the Main House? Like Ivan? And Xëri?"

"They might join us later on," Terra answered, "but for now, they're going to be helping out with preparations for the newcomers' arrivals."

In the span of an instant Brent remembered Aaron's mention of Jeffrey, and how he was due to be returning to the village that night. Connecting it to Terra's words, he figured that Jeffrey was to be entering Taranis with a crowd of rescued slaves in tow.

But even with that knowledge, he didn't like the idea of Ivan or Xëri having to miss out on the evening's events.

"What if they miss it?" he asked next. "Y'know, the…the Lu… Lumin…" He trailed off, not entirely sure he was saying the word right.

"Nah, they won't miss it." Ben swung Mekial onto his shoulders. "The Luminoro Watch lasts for a pretty long time. There's a lot of those things, y'know."

Brent frowned. "What things?"

"Dad!" Renée hissed, pressing a finger over her lips as she scowled at him. "It's supposed to be a secret!"

It was Ben's turn to frown. "What is?"

"The thing!"

"I don't get it."

"I think she's saying she doesn't want us to spoil it for Brent," Terra translated and she looked at her daughter with a soft smile. "That right?"

Renée nodded, pleased that her mother understood. "Yeah!"

"But why?" Both Brent and Ben blurted in unison, the first facing Renée and the latter Terra.

"You'll find out when you get there!" Renée told her new friend and after taking his hand in hers, she spun around and ran off. "Now c'mon, let's go!"

"Hey, wait up!" Aaron called, hurrying after them.

"Don't forget me!" Eklaire shouted, dashing at his heels.

"Where are we even going?" Brent managed as he was hauled off for the second time, and he forced himself to fall into step behind Renée so he wouldn't stumble and fall.

"To the lake!" she said over her shoulder. "That's where the Luminoro Watch is!" That said she led him into the valley with Aaron and Eklaire close behind.

As they went they were spotted by other children, who saw

their departure as a sign that it was time for them to do the same. So with cheers and yelling they hurried after them, chasing after or racing one another as they did.

Urged by the suddenness of their leave, the adults were forced to follow. Soon, all that had gathered at the foot of the main road were processing into the low-lying fields.

"Liam, if you want, you can go ahead," his sister told him as they followed the crowd.

He was holding her hand, wordlessly helping her along as they went, and he shook his head. "It's okay." He viewed her out of the side of his eye. "It's not like I won't be able to find them later. We're all going to the same place."

"One mature kid you got there, Laura," Ben said with half a smile. "Ours just grabbed a boy and took off!"

Laura giggled gently. "You make it sound like that's a bad thing."

"Well, it would be a problem if they were a bit older," Ben admitted with a thoughtful, upward tilt of his eyes.

Suddenly, Mekial slapped his hands over them.

Ben grunted in surprise. "What're you up to there, Mek?"

"I'm gonna be your eyes!" he said happily and he looked at the path before them. "Go straight!"

"This again?" Ben smiled and through the hole that Mekial had unwittingly made between his fingers, he viewed the way ahead. "All right, I'm gonna go straight!"

"And left!" Mekial said next, thinking he was the reason for Ben's successful avoidance of a collision with a villager.

"Going left," he agreed. As he fancifully spun around the woman he'd evaded, he saw fit to come clean. "By the way, you know I can see through your fingers, right?"

"What?!" Mekial hurriedly fixed his mistake.

"A-ah!" Ben staggered when his world went dark. "Careful, Mek, don't gouge my eyes out...!"

Behind them, Terra smiled.

Then, averting her gaze from her staggering husband, she looked at Laura. "So, it's gonna be soon, huh?"

"Hm?" Laura looked at her. When Terra nodded at her swollen

abdomen, she understood. "Oh, yes. Any day now." With her free hand, she rubbed her stomach tenderly. "Greta thinks it's going to be a lively child, because she keeps kicking me."

"'She'?" Terra echoed.

Laura laughed sheepishly. "Yeah…I'm hoping for a little girl." She smiled distantly. "I'm thinking to name her Lilian."

Liam glanced up at her. "That's a nice name."

His sister chuckled. "You say it so plainly, Liam. I don't think I believe you."

Liam looked at her out of the side of his eye and when he turned away, he was quiet for a second. Then he took a breath, and with a tone of heavily forced sincerity he said, "That's a nice name!"

Laura laughed again. "Now you just sound like you're trying too hard!"

"That's a really nice name," Liam tried again, and Laura's laughter quieted just a little.

"There you go! Thank you, Liam."

He smiled without showing his teeth, his silver gaze meeting hers out of the corner of his eye.

Terra, too, allowed a similar smile to tug at the sides of her lips. "I'm sure she'll be beautiful," she said. "Just like her mother."

Laura smiled back.

25

THE REMAINING WALK to the lake was short and unorganized. Here and there the older villagers talked with the children, sweeping them into the air or listening to them talk about their day, while elsewhere some walked in distracted solitude, only to be dragged into conversation by friends drawing near.

So no one was alone and with his hand still clasped in Renée's, Brent was no different. It wasn't until they'd nearly reached the lake did Aaron ask why they were still holding hands.

With her cheeks burning, Renée let go.

Brent sent her a questioning look.

At last they arrived at the wall of pine trees that bordered the lake and they passed through them to access it. As the older villagers flooded its shores, the children flushed to its edge. There, some of them kicked at the water or knelt down in order to study the pebbles that scraped their toes.

Grinning excitedly, Renée took Brent's hand again and pulled him to the ledge of land that jutted out over the water. There, she released him. When she did, he set his sights on the villagers.

Some of them were still searching for a spot from which they could view the lake amidst so many people. Before long some kind of pattern was made, with the shorter villagers moving to the front while the taller ones either sat or stood behind them. Some even climbed into trees.

Brent stared, impressed. Then, he dropped his gaze and watched as Aaron and Eklaire joined him and Renée on the ledge. Behind them, Liam was coming.

Looking beyond him Brent saw that Liam's sister, Renée's parents and Mekial had already gathered close to the lake. As he watched them, Ben removed Mekial from his shoulders.

Facing away, he raised his eyes to the sky next.

The sun was still sinking, searing the horizon with a blazing orange that was layered beneath a mesh of soft blues and violets. Hardly any clouds were seeable and any that did exist were just wisps that spanned the skyline.

A soft wind sighed against him and he cast his eyes over the lake.

It was still.

A second later the breeze died and when it did, he noticed that it had taken the villagers' voices with it.

He turned to see them.

They were all watching the lake, waiting.

He couldn't even hear crickets.

"What's going on?" He faced his friends.

"We've got the best seat in the house." Aaron's eyes were on the lake, but he spared a second to pass Brent a sideways look. "Just watch." He pointed at the water.

Brent looked at it again.

Nothing happened.

He frowned, puzzled. But before he could ask anything else, a golden light caught his attention.

It materialized over the lake's center and in the dying light of day, it shone brightly. It was small, no bigger than a fist, and from it there came a sharp jingling like a bell.

A series of wide ripples spread beneath it and as they expanded a second light appeared, blooming from the lake's shadowy depths to mount towards the surface.

Brent's eyes widened and as the light grew to consume the lake, a breath of awe escaped him.

With the increasing glow more golden lights began to appear, their forms rising from the heart of the lake to follow the first into the darkening sky.

Only a handful of them could be seen at the start and then more joined them, then more and more until at last, their numbers were too great to count. When it looked like thousands were rising from the water still more were popping out, hailing from every inch and corner until the entire lake was hidden beneath their divine illumination.[tv]

Soon, some of the lights began to rise feet away from where he and his friends were standing.

Startled, Brent took a step back.

Still, with such an up-close view he couldn't help but admire the way they maintained an air of grace and steadiness, moving in such a way that they seemed to be more drifting instead of ascending, like they were riding gentle currents that ferried them into the sky.

Tilting his head back, he watched as the lights nearest to the top peaked to a height that was level with the canopy of the trees. From there, their glow fell upon everything in the area, striking the trees, rocks and grass with such brilliance that it seemed as if they were emitting a surreal radiance of their own.

Enthralled, he continued to watch these lights, these climbing orbs of enchantment, and his lips parted with the start of a fascinated smile. It wasn't until a sudden ringing sounded did he snap out of his trance.

An instant later, an irregular movement flashed far above him.

Looking in that direction, he saw that some of the little balls of light were splitting from the rest, separating themselves until they had enough room to circle in the air. Just after doing so they dropped to soar towards those who were watching them, leaving a trail of glittering stardust in their wake.

When close enough they spiraled around the villagers with soft ringing and in response the villagers laughed or smiled, their faces shining in the luminescence that zipped around them.

Another commotion of tinkling struck his ears and after tearing his eyes from the villagers, Brent viewed the incredible swarm of lights in time to catch more of them break ranks.

His amazement now palpable, he watched them with an open-mouthed grin, then dropped his eyes to where he knew the lake's

NO JOKES FOR YOU
CODE: THELUMINORO

surface to be.

There, some of the lights were bouncing across the waters, forcing tiny waves to ripple towards the bank as they neared the shore.

One such orb did so repeatedly as it went along, bounding forth as if it was skipping, and upon reaching the slab of stone that Brent was standing on it shot up and into his line of sight.

His face dropped.

The light was a person.

Or it looked like one at least, with a humanoid body and eyes, even hair. But because of the bright light that encased it, it would've been impossible for him to tell unless he had this closer view.

He even got a better one: the little being flew nearer to his face and it was with startled realization that Brent noticed it was nude.

But its skin was just as gold as its light, so he couldn't see any finite details of its body. Still, its flat chest and wide shoulders lead him to conclude it was a male.

It flew closer, stopping shy of his nose.

At that point he saw that it had wings, which were fluttering so fast that he'd hardly noticed them before. It also lacked several features that he believed to be crucial to anyone's face. For instance it had no nose, nor did it have a mouth. It even lacked pupils and irises, leaving its eyes to look like cutouts in its golden skin.

Brent leaned back when the little man flew even closer.

Only when a distant laugh sounded behind him did he peek away and in so doing, he saw that yet more of these little beings had descended to fly around the villagers. Even his friends were being acknowledged by them.

He turned away, moving to reface the one that had been observing him, and he found that it'd been joined by several more.

There were males and females now and like their male counterparts, the feminine figures were clothed in a light that hid the details of their matured anatomy.

They all jolted back as soon as he faced them, startled by the unpredicted turning of his head. But then they pulled in close again, scrutinizing him with their empty eyes.

Brent retreated, but they covered the distance he'd formed with one single, collective motion.

Unsure as to how else he could regain his personal space he wound up standing there, bent into an awkward leaning position as the glowing creatures continued to examine him.

What did they want?

"They're talking to you," he heard Aaron say and, confused, he whipped around to look at him.

"What?"

"You can't hear them?" Aaron asked, raising his eyebrows, and the glowing creatures that were surrounding him parted so he could approach.

"I…" Brent looked at his audience and strained his ears to pick up the sound of voices.

But besides those of his friends and the other villagers, he could only hear the same gentle tinkling that he'd heard when the lights had first arrived.

"Maybe it's cuz you just met 'em," Aaron guessed, spying Brent's hesitance. "Here, I'll translate!" He eyed the jingling lights carefully. "They're asking for your name."

"My name?" Brent cast Aaron a sideways glance. "Um…I'm Brent."

Gentle ringing filled his ears.

"That one said it's a cool name," Aaron said, pointing at the one that had first come to greet Brent. "He says his name's Silas."

"How do you know what they're saying?" Brent asked, turning to Aaron again.

He raised a shoulder. "Every Avat can hear what they're saying. Even half-Avats, like me. Maybe you have to train yourself or something."

Brent looked at the floating beings again. "What are these things, anyway?"

"They're the Luminoro!" Aaron answered. "They live beneath the lake. But every summer they migrate to the Adriak Mountains. Then they come back here in the fall."

"Why do they do that?"

Aaron scratched his head. "Um…I think it's cuz they don't like how hot it gets down here in the summer."

"Yeah, that's right." Liam joined their conversation, appearing at Brent's left side. "They like cool, wet environments. Lakes in the Adriak Mountains give them that in the summer, then they come back here in the fall, when the heat's not as bad."

"Did they tell you that?" Brent looked at him while pointing at the Luminoro.

"No. We learned that from Yulia."

Brent blinked, remembering that Yulia was their teacher at the schoolhouse. He probably hadn't been around for that lesson.

At the sound of another chorus of ringing, Liam fixed his eyes on the Luminoro.

He refaced his blue-haired friend. "They want to know where you're from."

"I'm from…" Brent stopped, but then decided that there could be no harm in telling the truth. "The city."

Something like recognition flashed in Liam's eyes. "You mean Axelius?"

"Um…yeah," Brent replied.

He hadn't referred to the city by its name in years. It had become irrelevant to him, what with everything else he'd been concerned about while living on the streets. It felt strange to hear its proper title again, especially when he was so far from it.

"Huh." Liam looked at the ringing Luminoro. "They wanna know why your hair's blue if you're from this province."

Brent frowned. "Huh?"

"Wow, you didn't learn anything in the city, huh?" Aaron almost looked surprised. "Y'know how the Empire's divided up, right? Each part is a province. Lenora is the one east of here, where Eklaire's from. It's why she and her mom have white hair even though they're not old, remember? I heard some people even have green or pink hair over there.

"But you said you're not from there." He furrowed his eyebrow skeptically. "So, they wanna know why your hair's so different anyway."

"Oh. Um…" Brent hesitated. "I-I don't know."

Aaron made a small humming sound of thought, then switched his sight to the Luminoro when they voiced yet more words that Brent couldn't understand. "That one likes it, though. She says it reminds her of the sky."

Brent looked up and patted his unruly locks. "Uh, thanks."

"Hmmm…"

Brent directed his eyes to Liam next. He looked like he was thinking about something. "What?"

"Nothing." Liam withdrew from his thoughts with a shake of his head. "I was just wondering why you couldn't hear them talk, that's all."

"Oh." Brent rubbed one of his ears distractedly. After a moment, he looked up again. "So…why do they glow?"

"They're connected to the aether," Aaron said unflinchingly. "Isn't it obvious?"

Brent lifted his eyebrows, almost disturbed. "The…aether?"

"What?" Aaron's face opened in disappointment, his brow creasing. "Don't tell me you don't know what that is, either…"

Brent shrunk back and the Luminoro closed in on him, curious. He suddenly felt self-conscious. "Well, I mean…I know what it is, but…"

His mind rewound, shooting him into the past for the shortest of moments: standing in the midst of a wide, gold-gilded chamber built especially for training; holding his hands out, feeling for the touch of something that he couldn't see or hear, or even feel; the strain of reaching for it, hoping for that something to connect with him —

Then the blast of defiant energy that had ignited in front of his hands, blowing him off his feet, and the scowl of disdain that he'd received from the man who'd been watching him…

He slid out of the recollection, troubled by all of the negativity that it struck him with. "I…tried to use it once," he said quietly. "But I couldn't."

"Oh." Aaron didn't really wear any kind of reaction to go along with his response.

Liam didn't even say anything.

Brent righted himself. "Uh…guess I just don't really know how it works."

Withdrawing, the Luminoro chimed noisily.

Liam regarded him with a troubled look.

"Oh boy…" Aaron rubbed his forehead.

Brent glanced between them, annoyed now. "Well, it's not like I've never seen people use it! I just…don't really know a lot about it."

"It's like…um…" Aaron thought for a second. "It's what binds the whole world together. You know: people, animals, the elements, plants…everything." He paused. "You've heard of aetheriests before, right?"

"Well, yeah." Brent straightened a little. "They're the people who can use the aether. And I've heard of The Aether Circus. And you said there's some here in Taranis. Also…" He thought for a second, his gaze dipping in contemplation. "There were a lot of them in the city…the really good ones were used for security, but only in certain places so I didn't see them a lot. The ones who aren't so great operate some of the ferry boats, I think. And other stuff."

"Good, you know that much at least." Aaron was relieved. "You're right: aetheriests are people who can connect to the aether. So they can do all kinds of crazy stuff, like manipulate water or earth to fight, or create shields, or move stuff without touching it… Yulia says that everyone's got the potential to connect to it, because we're all born with this stuff called, uh…" He racked his brain. "Adolescence! Yeah that's it."

"Quintessence," Liam amended without looking at him.

Aaron pinked. "Anyway, that's what everything is made of. Aetheriests are people who've learned to tap into that energy and link it to the aether. Then they reach through the aether to connect to other things and do crazy stuff with them.

"But the Luminoro are born with so much" — he glanced at Liam — "quintessence that they're just always connected to the aether. So they can do weird stuff without even trying. Like glow." He watched as one of the tiny creatures circled around his face and settled atop his shoulder. Tossing his gaze back to Brent, he concluded, "They're small, but a lot of people think the Luminoro are even stronger than the most skilled aetheriests. It's almost like the aether is living inside them." His face lit up. "They're kind of like aetherians!"

"What?" Brent was confused.

An aetherian?

He'd never heard *that* before.

"Oh. So you *don't* know about that." Aaron hadn't meant to sound condescending, but his words stung Brent anyway. "Aetherians are the strongest kinds of aetheriests. I've heard villagers tell stories that you can tell who an aetherian is just by looking at their eyes. They're supposed to be this glow-y, greenish-blue, kinda gold-looking…"

"They're unnatural," Liam clarified to Brent's slowly deepening frown. "Apparently, you can't mistake them when you see one."

"Oh," Brent said. "So, if anyone can connect to the aether and become an aetheriest or an aetherian, can everyone in Taranis do it?"

"No…" Aaron's face soured and the Luminoro that had perched upon him fluttered away. "We only have a few aetheriests here — like, five. And a lot of the villagers have already gotten too involved in certain trades to bother becoming an aetheriest. By now, it'd slow everything down if they tried to learn. Everyone else is an Avat and if you have Avat blood in you, you can't connect to the aether at all. Guess that's why you failed at it before. Not sure why you even bothered though. Everyone knows Avats can't use it."

Brent frowned, perplexed. "Why not?"

Aaron seemed bothered by the topic. "It's complicated."

Brent's eyes dropped, his frown steady and pensive, but sour.

While what Aaron had just said certainly explained his failure at using the aether, he didn't like the idea that it had happened just because he was part-Avat. It was as if it scorned him as much as the Empire did.

His resentment was cast aside when the Luminoro suddenly chimed and scattered as streaks of light.

He looked up with a start. "Where're they going?"

"They wanted to go and say hi to some other people before they leave, I guess," Aaron said, watching them shoot off. "But they said, 'It's very nice to meet you, Brent.' They wanna talk to you again when they come back."

"Uh…huh…" Brent replied faintly, his eyes still on the departing beings.

Hearing familiar laughter, he dropped his eyes and looked to his left.

There Renée, Eklaire and a younger child were standing ankle-deep in the lake with several Luminoro flying around them.

At first glance Brent thought the third person was Mekial, but upon a harder look he saw that this child, although small like Mekial, was actually a darker-skinned female that was younger than the company she stood in. Her clothes were also tattered and a pair of pointy ears stuck out of her scraggly black hair.

Even though he'd only been in Taranis for a week, Brent didn't recognize her.

As that thought crossed his mind, Aaron said something that clarified his confusion, "Looks like some of the newcomers have come down."

Brent threw his eyes to the shore and saw that the number of people on the bank had multiplied. Many of the new faces were dressed in clothes that didn't resemble the attire of the typical villager, and so he guessed that they were the slaves who'd just been brought to Taranis.

If that was true, then that meant…

"Jeffrey!" Aaron cried, confirming Brent's incomplete thought and following his line of sight, Brent spotted the man he was referring to.

With his arms folded he was talking to Richter, and was tall and dark-skinned with a battle-toned physique and narrowed eyes. His ears were also round, a feature that was obvious thanks to there being no hair on his perfectly shaved head, and with his face cut into a deep frown Brent wondered what he and Richter were talking about.

His curiosity was short-lived though, because when Aaron and Liam went to greet him his dark expression vanished. It was such a casual transition that he actually seemed as approachable as anyone else.

Even so Brent didn't join them, because he soon recalled that Jeffrey was their sparring instructor. Reluctant to enter into conversation with him, he chose to head towards his female companions instead.

Eklaire was the first to see him coming.

"Brent!" She waved gleefully. "Ain't this just so cool? Bet yer glad we kept this one a secret, huh?" She winked her green eye shut when one of the Luminoro bumped into her cheek.

"Was it a good surprise?" Renée asked as he joined them. "Xëri wanted you to enjoy it. She said she hoped it'd help you get used to the valley more."

"Yeah…it's cool." Brent watched the Luminoro that were around them. "Do you know what they're saying?"

"Well, no." Renée smiled bashfully. "Non-Avats can't hear them. We usually have Aaron or Liam translate."

"But since they ain't here, we got our new pal Harver here to translate for us!" Eklaire held a hand out to the girl that Brent had noticed from afar.

He looked at her for the first time since his arrival.

She already had her big round eyes on him. In fact, she was staring fixedly at his blue hair.

"Harver, this here's our buddy, Brent!" Eklaire told her. "He's new, too. Showed up last week!"

Harver looked from her to Brent.

She didn't say anything.

"Hi," Brent tried.

Harver was tight-lipped.

"She's kinda shy," Eklaire admitted. "But look! She said this one's name is Clara." She pointed at one of the Luminoro who, upon seeing Brent, whizzed towards his face.

"Hello," he said, still unused to how the beings so eagerly invaded his comfort zone.

The creature jingled in response.

"And that there's Illius!" Eklaire went on. "And Fon, and Dalia…" She was now indicating the one who'd crashed into her cheek. "She's a bit of a klutz, if ya ask me. I think she's still tryin' to get a hang of those wings of hers!"

"They all kinda look alike…" Brent mumbled.

"Aw, c'mon! Ya just gotta look real hard!"

"It's okay, Brent." Renée smiled as some of the Luminoro near her sat on her head and shoulders. "There's a lot of them to keep track of after all." She looked pointedly at the lake.

Brent did the same and much to his amazement, he found that Luminoro were still rising from the water to join the vast number that were hovering above the treetops.

They were circling slowly there and for the first time that night, he realized that this was an event that the villagers were used to seeing. It was almost hard to believe that now that he lived with them he, too, was going to be able to see it as often as it happened.

Just the thought of having something like this in his future made him glad. He couldn't think of anything he'd seen that he could compare it to. There was nothing in the city that radiated such a natural beauty. There wasn't even anything in the imperial fields that could stand up to it.

But at the same time, he couldn't help but feel that there was something…familiar about it.

With his eyes on the sparkling cloud of creatures, he pondered that notion for a moment, wondering why it would ever occur to him.

At last, he uncovered the reason: the warm light was reminiscent of the glow that had surrounded Adelle's grave when he'd first visited it. It was as if, even now, she was here.

A soft smile tugged on his lips.

Suddenly, he saw fit to lower his gaze and almost instantly, he found himself looking at Renée.

Or, to be more precise, he found her looking at him.

Why was she looking at him?

He made to frown but before he could she jumped, startled by their abrupt eye contact, and whipped her face away. She did it so fast that the Luminoro on her head had to cling to her hair to keep from flying off.

He viewed her profile for a second and by light of the ascending Luminoro, he saw that her lips were pressed taut and her shoulders were stiff. A shade of red had also filled her golden-brown cheeks.

Was she sick?

"Are you okay?" he asked.

She flinched and spun to face him. "Y-yeah! I'm okay."

Brent wasn't sure if he should believe her. But the longer he looked at her, the more a certain question burned within him. "…Can I ask you something?"

"Yeah, what?"

"I was just wondering…why you wanted to be a raider."

Eklaire looked from him to Renée.

Harver glanced between them. It wasn't all that hard to tell she didn't know what his question was about.

"…Because…Mom and Dad do it," Renée answered after a pause and Eklaire raised her eyebrows, her mouth forming a soundless "ooh" of intrigue.

"Not to help people?" Brent asked, his tone one of interest.

"Of course I wanna help people!" Renée replied. "But, I wanna be like Mom and Dad, too. To be strong like them and to protect people like them." She fell silent and her face of resolve reverted to one of uncertainty. "Does that…sound weird?"

Brent opened his mouth to reply, but then he stopped himself.

"I think it's great!" Eklaire exclaimed, throwing her arms skyward.

Renée smiled at her appreciatively and she looked at Brent again. "Why'd you ask?"

"Because…uh…" He threw his eyes to the side, then turned back to the Luminoro. "Just wondering."

Renée eyed him carefully, then blinked curiously when he decided to add something else.

"Or I guess…I still don't get it," he admitted and his gaze became distant. "Why even Avats want to be raiders. We can't even use the aether…"

Eklaire puckered her brow sadly.

Harver, clinging to the front of her raggedy shirt, simply looked between the older children with her big, round eyes.

"Hmm…I don't know about that."

Eyebrows lifted, Brent looked at Renée suddenly.

The girl herself tied her hands behind her hips and looked up at the cloud of Luminoro as they continued to climb out of the lake.

"Y'know, sometimes we perform plays with the other kids from the schoolhouse," she told him. "Every year, we put on a show at the Feast of Liberty, when we celebrate the day that Chief Ivan and

Lady Xëri first built the village. A few times, we've performed shows with Avat aetherians." She faced Brent with a twinkle in her eye and beamed. "Like Zion the Hero!"

"Zion?" Brent echoed and he shifted so that his entire body was facing her. "The 'Hero'?"

"Yup!"

"Ooh, those plays're so fun!" Eklaire exclaimed, pumping her fists, and her burst of excitement caused Harver to look up at her. "He was the strongest aetherian to every walk the continent, before the Empire! He went'n saved everyone from these nasty monsters that were tearin' everythin' up! I reckon nothin' would even exist right now if it wudn't fer what he did."

Harver seemed intrigued by this.

Brent couldn't hide his interest, either. "He did that?"

"Does a cat have climbin' gear?!"

"Uh…"

"The answer's 'yes', silly!"

"O-oh."

"I get why a lot of Avats say that they can't use the aether," Renée said, drawing their conversation back to the topic at hand. "It seems like none of them can. I've never met an Avat aetheriest, either. But" — she perked up — "why can't there be another Zion? Or maybe there already is one somewhere out there! And maybe," she smiled, "we'll get to meet them someday!"

Brent could only stare at her in answer, stunned by her optimism and at the same time, inspired by it.

"If we get to meet another Zion, I'm gonna bake him the best Arkanian Prune Pie he ever had!" Eklaire cheered, jumping forth to stand next to Renée, who turned her bright smile to her. The little Lenoran grinned back. "We'll have a whole party!"

Renée nodded. "Yeah!"

Something like tiny bells rang in her ears, and she turned to the Luminoro that were still around her.

The ones that had sat on her were floating away now and those that'd been in Eklaire and Harver's company were doing the same.

"Awww! Is it time for them to leave already?" Eklaire asked Harver.

"That's…what they're saying," the Avat girl answered, her voice as timid as her hair was wild. "They said that…they have to meet up with their families and go now. But…" She paused as more tinkling was fed into their ears. "They said…that they'll come and see us again, when they come back in the fall."

At the conclusion of her translation the creatures chimed melodically, and with a flash of light they took off to join their relatives.

"Buh-bye!" Eklaire called, waving her arms over her head.

More ringing sounded around them and Brent twisted to see the shore just as the Luminoro that had been with the other villagers began to take their leave as well.

The villagers waved to them, as did the children, and the last of the Luminoro broke free of the lake.

As their light left it the waters darkened, returning to their colorless state, and up above the Luminoro made one last circle, their shrill voices swallowing the night air.

Then they flew away, a big cloud of sparkling light that soared towards Taranis and to the mountains beyond.

Brent continued to stare after them as their light faded in the sky. He didn't look away even when it vanished altogether.

"Pretty neat, huh?" Eklaire asked, walking to his side as she too, stared at the starlit heavens. "Mama says they travel through the aether at some point to make their trip faster. I can't wait to see 'em when they get back!"

Brent lowered his eyes to her. The Luminoro traveled *through* the aether?

They really were incredible.

"Um…I'm, I'm gonna go now," Harver mumbled meekly and with a series of small splashes she sprinted out of the water and to Jeffrey, where she huddled close to his side.

Brent couldn't tell if Jeffrey was upset or just indifferent when he saw her, having glanced away from the villager that he was talking to before returning to their conversation.

"Poor thing!" Eklaire said, having also seen Harver glue herself to the raider. "She's stickin' closer to Jeffrey than white on rice!"

Brent squinted at her.

Eklaire noticed. So she thrust her arm out in gesture to Harver. "It's like she's stuck to his side!"

"O-oh."

"Eklaire says weird stuff sometimes," Renée said, having overheard the exchange.

"Right…"

"It's how I talk!" Eklaire huffed. "Still, I feel bad…Jeffrey wanted us to play with her, but Harver's just so shy!"

"Brent was shy, too!" Renée reminded her and Brent blushed. "I'm sure Harver'll come around. We just gotta keep trying!"

"Just like we did with Brent!" Eklaire slung her arm around his shoulder and pulled him close, making him grunt. "Sure did turn out to be a great guinea pig, huh?"

"I'm not a pig!" Brent retorted.

"That's just another one of Eklaire's weird sayings," Renée laughed.

Eklaire did too.

Brent didn't join in.

But when Eklaire snorted he had to and they wound up laughing together.

"What's so funny?" someone behind them asked and they turned to see Ben approaching. "I want in!"

"Eklaire snorted," Renée giggled.

Eklaire, who was still laughing, snorted again. So she started laughing harder.

"She's laughing at herself!" Renée said through her mirth, holding her stomach. "Breathe, Eklaire!"

Eklaire sighed and wiped the tears from her eyes. "Okay…I'm okay…"

They seemed to calm down.

But when Brent made a snorting sound to imitate Eklaire, they started laughing all over again.

"So! The quiet kid's got a sense of humor after all!" Ben tousled Brent's hair and the boy grinned. "I like that! Comin' outta your shell!"

Brent laughed and pushed his hand away. "Okay, okay! Stop!" He pat his hair back into place.

"C'mon, I made it better! Almost as good as mine!" Ben narrowed his eyes and looked off into the distance, and he smoothed the edges of his hair with a slow and dramatic movement. "How d'you like it, Ren? Been trying out some new gel."

Renée laughed. "It looks the same, Dad!"

"What? Naww," Ben waved a hand as if her statement were preposterous and Renée's smile widened. "Y'think? Maybe I should make a new gel." He grabbed her around the waist and sat her atop his shoulders. "Still think it smells like flowers?"

"Always!"

"Definitely need a new gel, then. Flowers are girly."

"Dad!"

Ben laughed and he looked at Brent and Eklaire. "Well, the others've already started to head back. And hey, your mother's taken my suggestion for dinner!" he added, his eyes glittering with humor, and he tilted his head to Renée. "Tonight, we're having toad legs and cricket feet!"

The children wrinkled their noses in distaste. "Eww!"

"Oh, it's not that bad. Healthy even!" Ben brushed off jokingly and with Brent and Eklaire beside him, he started away from the lake's edge and trekked further inland.

The other villagers who'd been standing close to the shoreline moved to do the same, distancing themselves from the still waters as they headed towards the road that would guide them back to Taranis. Here, there and everywhere parents took hold of their children's hands or carried the smaller ones on their shoulders, while in other places some chose to linger and take part in small but lighthearted conversation.

"We should have wild hen instead!" Renée exclaimed as they passed through the diminishing crowd. "Like the ones you caught earlier!"

Ben laughed. "You want me to hunt for more right now? They're probably all hiding!"

"What about soup?" Renée tried next, eagerly leaning forward to peer into her father's eyes. "With the bread that me and Mom made earlier!"

"Hey, now *that* sounds tasty…!"

Their voices softened then, fading with their distancing forms.

Behind them Brent suddenly stopped, his attention caught by someone who was watching him from nearby.

It was Harver.

And she was alone.

With Renée, Eklaire and Ben drifting away he glanced about, expecting to see Jeffrey.

But the only ones in sight were a handful of departing villagers. Not one of them noticed him or the dark-eyed child that was staring at him.

So, presuming that she'd been separated from Jeffrey, he figured he should take her back to Taranis himself.

Firmly set on this he made his way towards her, one hand reaching out, and at the same time he opened his mouth to verbally offer the aid that he meant to give.

Before he could, she spoke.

"I…I remember you," she said, her eyes never leaving his. "You…you're from the mansion, in the city." She reached up to seize clumps of her ratty tunic and her shoulders hunched upward. "You're…the son of Viceroy Diomedes. You're a prince."

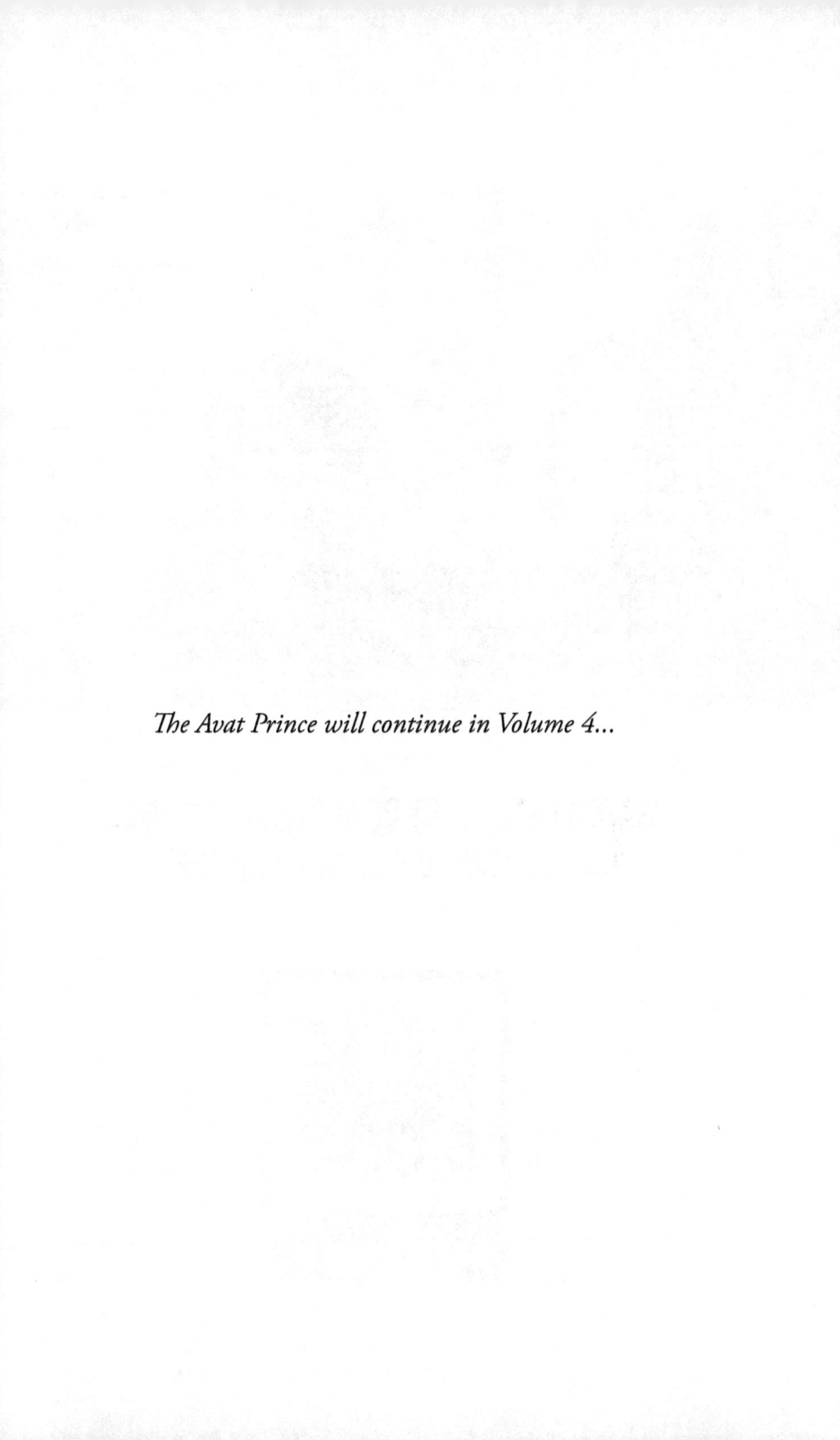

The Avat Prince will continue in Volume 4...

TALES OF ARKANIA
new episodes every 3rd Saturday

WATCH <u>FREE TALES OF ARKANIA EPISODES</u> ON THE MVP TV YOUTUBE CHANNEL!

Brand-new bonus content for *The Avat Prince* every third Saturday!

Featuring an international cast of voice talent, including award-winning VA Josh Portillo!

THE AVAT PRINCE: VOLUME 4

EMPYREAN'S LIKENESS STOOD atop the archway that led to Lyrik Estate, its golden form gleaming like fire in the setting sun's light. With its beak wide and wingtips stretched to the clouds it scowled over the city of Axelius, horns erect in preparation of flight and its talons flexed against its pedestal.

The viceroy's royal carriage traveled beneath it, its high wheels of gold rolling over the paved path that made up the underlying roadway and the cul-de-sac that it led to. Surrounded by its security detail the carriage stopped there, at the edge of a vast walkway that led to the mansion.

One of the foot soldiers that had been walking alongside it opened the side door and stepped aside.

Viceroy Diomedes slipped out of its cushioned interior first and moved aside for his daughter to do the same. As soon as her feet touched the ground, he proceeded to guide her down the tree-lined path and back to their abode.

A unit of soldiers broke away from the carriage and walked two-by-two in front of them, their red and blue uniforms a stark contrast against the stone path and greenery of the front yard gardens. Their weapons were even more distinct, for each of them were equipped with the same heavy shield and blade, or a spear-lance and bow.

The mansion that the group approached was a massive stone

building whose great height was level with that of Empyrean's statue at its gate. From the crown of its only watchtower a flagpole ascended, and at its peak there billowed a banner, upon which the face of the chief deity flapped menacingly. A few floors above the main entrance there was also a wide wall window, whose shadowed interior extended over the entryway where it was supported by ionic columns.

Once the viceroy and his daughter reached the square plot of land where the entire mansion sat, their security officers broke ranks to form a path for them. They stood still as the royal family members passed between them.

"Hail, Your Highness!" the two guards stationed at the front doors cried when Diomedes and his daughter were close. They clapped their fists to their breasts and slammed their ankles together.

Viceroy Diomedes lifted a hand, permitting them to stand at ease.

They did.

"We pray your travels went well, Highness," said the one on the right.

"Just another full week of meetings and political discourse," Diomedes responded vaguely and he and his daughter stopped as the second guard opened the doors for them. "Nothing was amiss. I'm only glad that Adiné at least got to see the ocean."

His daughter, clinging to his hand, smiled.

"Good to hear, Sire. Also," the soldier seemed to shift uncomfortably, "you have an unannounced guest."

"Oh?" Diomedes' gaze drifted to the entrance hall of his mansion once the doors were ajar.

A glittering chandelier decorated the marble room with spots of light and on either wall, a set of polished stairs spiraled to the upper floors. Straight ahead, the hall connected to the deeper portions of the mansion.

Standing in the very center of this corridor was another soldier, his silver armor gilded with gold emblems and crafty embellishments. A thick red cape hung about his large shoulders and with his helmet tucked beneath his arm, he regarded the viceroy with a somber frown.

Diomedes entered the hall wordlessly, Adiné still at his side. His face was expressionless.

"Welcome back, Your Highness." The soldier bowed.

"Margrave Regal Inkert," Diomedes greeted and behind him the magnificent doors of the Estate were shut. "I'm tired. I hope you have a good reason for showing up without a summons."

"I do, Sire." Margrave Regal raised his head, his rough face still cut into that same, dour expression. "It regards Renthor, Your Highness."

CONTINUE READING IN
THE AVAT PRINCE: VOLUME 4!

About the Author(ess)

Myranda V. Peterson

A young artist who wears many hats, Myranda Victoria Peterson is an author, illustrator, animator and voice director with a contagious passion for storytelling. She first started off writing plays, which her parents and friends helped her perform when she was a little girl. A self-taught artist, her creative work is heavily inspired by anime and Japanese pop culture. She creates original, high-fantasy content that aims to inspire the youth of today with themes of generosity, courage, friendship and hope.

Myranda is the founder and CEO of the independent imprint and joint animation studio House MVP and lives in Boston, where many famous, classic authors have gone before her. She hopes that one day, her name will join them!